Here's what others are saying about *Evolution of an Xmas Letter:*

"Our Christmas Letter this year is a book? Are you kidding me? A book? What were *you* thinking?"~*Wendy Coile*

"Always, always, always keep holiday letters to two-pages or less. People have cookies to bake and don't want to be bored to tears reading every little itty-bitty, teeny-weeny, miniscule detail of your life."~*Prof. Vicki Meade, Adjunct Writing Professor at three big name colleges that don't want to be mentioned here*

"Drop the plum pudding! Put down the silver eggnog cup! Leave your presents under the tree and leave the turkey on 'low'! Forget '*Twas The Night Before Christmas* and instead read aloud your copy of *Evolution of an Xmas Letter*. You'll laugh! You'll cry (well, maybe not *cry*)! But you will love it!"~*Yoda*

"Smiley face, plus, plus!"~*Wendy Sand Eckel, Famous Novelist*

"A thorough examination of the torrid trials and tribulations, daring to peer deeply into every crevice of human experience. A riveting tale to be read by firelight, a bottle of Château Margaux 1995 by your side, on Christmas Eve with a heavy snow falling and the electricity out of service."~*Mary Bargteil, Muse by birth and Excavator of Creative Writing by profession*

"The Christmas book Jon Coile's reading public have been waiting for. Stack it up with other masterpieces such as Dickens' *Christmas Story* or Dylan Thomas', *A Child's Christmas in Wales*....vintage Coile."~*Joe Nold, Ancient Mariner.*

"Poor Wendy."~*Suzanne Gingher*

"If you only read one page of this entire book, make sure it is the last page and you read it before noon on January 1st!"~*Drew Elioc, Notorious Critic*

Evolution of an Xmas Letter

Evolution of an Xmas Letter

Holiday Greetings from Jon & Wendy

(The Unabridged Edition)

Jon & Wendy Coile

Lynn,
Merry Christmas!
Jon & Wendy

iUniverse, Inc.
New York Lincoln Shanghai

Evolution of an Xmas Letter
Holiday Greetings from Jon & Wendy

iUniverse books may be ordered through booksellers or by contacting:

iUniverse
2021 Pine Lake Road, Suite 100
Lincoln, NE 68512
www.iuniverse.com
1-800-Authors (1-800-288-4677)

All the events in this book are based on the truth. But, so we don't become the first people ever sued for their Christmas Letter, we are now going to say that it's all fiction. Any resemblance to persons living or dead, and especially if you think you are one of the ignorant jerks portrayed in any incident described in these pages, is purely coincidental.

ISBN-13: 978-0-595-37849-4 (pbk)
ISBN-13: 978-0-595-67576-0 (cloth)
ISBN-13: 978-0-595-82222-5 (ebk)
ISBN-10: 0-595-37849-8 (pbk)
ISBN-10: 0-595-67576-X (cloth)
ISBN-10: 0-595-82222-3 (ebk)

Printed in the United States of America

To our family and friends who politely keep their real opinions of our holiday letter to themselves.

Acknowledgements

Holiday letters like this wouldn't happen without lots of encouragement from various quarters. We are indebted to a number of people and will do our best to acknowledge them here. First and foremost, Lauri Ladd, Marketing Director of Champion Realty pretends that she enjoys the annual project as much as we do, and contributes both creative guidance and fantastic artwork to give our Xmas Letters a semi-professional appearance.

Our family has a hand in the creation, either through feedback on the writing, or by participating in some of the antics that make it into the letter: A comprehensive family tree would be over the top but we would be very remiss if we failed to acknowledge the key players in no particular order: Russell Coile, Ellen Coile, Jennifer Coile, John Robrock & Sienna Coile Robrock, Andrew Coile, Chris & Susan Coile, Gloria Barton, Dick Barton, Eli Barton, Noelle & Blaise DeFazio, Dick, Sr. & Jacqie Barton, Chris & Pam Barton, Lori Coile & Gary, Courtney Coile, Henry Roman & Nathanial Coile Roman, Zachary Coile & Victoria, Peg Wallace, Nancy Coile, Walt & Helen Cone, Nessly, Sue & David Craig, Thelma McLachlan, The Veales, and cousins Diane, Kevin, Jamie & Kaleigh Greening in England.

For the writing, if it amuses, it was probably tweaked by my extremely creative writer friends who are in critique groups or other writing forums with me: Mary Bargteil, Shirley Bauer, Wendy Sand Eckel, Cindy Polansky Gallagher, Denny Kleppick, Vicki Meade, Susan Moger, Joe Nold, Pat O'Connell and Bridget Bell Webber. If the attempt at humor falls flat it is either because I didn't run it past them first, or failed to follow their advice.

As Stephen King put it in his masterpiece, *On Writing—A Memoir of the Craft*, when you write, you write for your "Ideal Reader". Our Ideal Readers are our family mentioned above, and our friends on our Christmas Card list. It is our attempt to entertain our Ideal Reader that keeps this writing exercise going. Some of these friends date back all the way to our youth. Some were met at work. Some are from our professional associations and others we met while in the pursuit of hobbies and recreation. In an uncharacteristic move to conserve space we will not list everybody on our list here, but please know that we are thinking of you and treasure your friendship.

Happy Holidays,

Jon & Wendy Coile
Osprey Point
December 25th, 2005

Chapter 1

A Book

If you are serial readers of our annual Xmas missive, you know that this is a classic example of a holiday tradition that has spun horribly out of control. You may be wondering how reconnecting every December with our family and friends evolved into these increasingly more ludicrous displays of the Holiday Letter genre.

To bring you up to speed, in case you are a new addition to our Christmas Mailing List, back in our first year of this cycle of holiday excess we put out an eight-page letter. Next our letter grew to a 32-page booklet, topped the following year by 48-pages of Haiku. With my wife, Wendy, strongly encouraging me to cut back to one page, last year's effort was a single sheet of BluePrint® rolled into a bright red tube. Thirty six inches by twenty four inches of ammonia reeking Xmas cheer. The BluePrint® raised the bar for unique holiday greetings.

How could I top that for this year, and more importantly, how did this holiday duty, traditionally feared by writer and readers alike, get to this point in the first place?

Well, sit back, grab a glass of eggnog and a frosted snowman cookie and settle in for a long read as I tell you the story of the *Evolution of an Xmas Letter*. It all started forty eight years ago, in the lush tropical paradise of Oahu in the Hawaiian Island chain...

Chapter 2

Fruitcake

"Oh, get over yourself!" Wendy said, as she glanced at the first few words appearing on the screen. "Hawaii? This year we're sending a book? Are you nuts? Last year's BluePrint® was wacky enough. Now you're embarrassing me, and yourself."

"But snookums, you'll be listed as the co-author on the Bowker's 'Books-In-Print' database. When people search Amazon.com for a good holiday book, like Grisham's *Skipping Christmas*, our Xmas Letter will pop up as co-written by you. How cool is that? Wendy Coile and John Grisham returned by the same Google search! You'll be famous."

"Infamous, maybe."

"Seriously, I don't think I have much of a choice this year. Our letter has taken on a life of its own and now our friends have started to look forward to see how we are going to try and top last year's effort. I knew that the BluePrint® would be hard to beat. I can't go backwards to a 48-page booklet now. I've got to go all the way—one direction or the other. It's either a book or fruitcake."

"I vote for fruitcake."

"Yuk, yuk."

"No, really. We can get them by the case at Wal-Mart."

"Now you are making stuff up. You've never shopped for fruitcake by the case, let alone at Wal-Mart."

"But I bet they have it."

"The other reason I want to make our letter into a book," I typed into the computer, ignoring my fruitcake wife, "is that 2005 is supposed to be the 'Year of the Book' for the Coile family."

"I'm right here. Reading over your shoulder. Did you forget?"

"The other reason I want to make our letter into a book," I typed, ignoring my lovely and charming wife, the woman of my dreams, the love of my life, the Yin to my...

"Knock it off!"

"...is that 2005 is supposed to be the 'Year of the Book' for the Coile family."

I was referring to a commitment several members of my family made last Christmas. We were celebrating the posthumous publication of my eldest brother's golf murder mystery, *Murder at Pebble Beach*, by R.C. Coile, Jr., released by iUniverse in hard cover and paperback in time for Christmas 2004. (Insert Shameless Plug Here: **Now Available on Amazon.com!**) With Russ' book quickly selling over 100 copies, the other would-be authors in the family, all with partially finished projects waiting patiently to be completed, decided that this was our year-of-the-book. We would buckle down, finish our final rewrites, and get our books out there in bookstores, on Barnes&Noble.com, and everywhere else Ingram's distribution arms reached.

I hit the ground running in January, sporadically but intensely working on my Intracoastal Waterway adventure sea story that I started writing in 1997 when I made the trip with my then 80-year-old father. He is now age-88 and still waiting to read the finished book. I knew I needed to get on it, and pronto.

Simultaneously with my attempts at writing, Wendy and I were immersed in building the house that we mentioned in last year's Xmas Letter. As the 'Year-of-the-Book' transformed for me into the 'Year-of-the-House-Under-Painstakingly-Slow-But Meticulously-Perfect-Construction-That-Seemed-Like-It-Would-Never-End' it quickly became apparent that, while this might be my year-of-the-book, it wasn't going to be the year of the *waterway* book. I needed a fallback plan.

I dug in the deep recesses of my mind, where my brain has indelibly catalogued every positive thing anyone has ever said about my writing, and searched for a little tidbit I knew was in there. It slowly percolated its way to the top. A casual comment, more than a year earlier.

"We love your holiday letter." Jeff Miller said, as he cashed my check to purchase The Moose, our then new-to-us twenty-year-old motorhome. "I wish there was someplace I could tell people to go to get a copy."

That was it. Publish a book and sell it on Amazon.com. I could cut-and-paste together 35,000 words from previous Xmas letters, write a few lines of fresh stuff to tie it all together, chop it into Dan Brownesque bite-size chapters and see if Jeff was just being overly flattering or if there really was a market for my prose. Plus I'd meet my familial commitment to publish something during the Coile Family "Year-of-the-Book."

Now if I can just keep from putting my readers to sleep, I thought, as I prepared to take them back with me forty-eight years, to the lush tropical paradise of Oahu in the Hawaiian Island chain...

Wait, wait, wait! I know better than to end a chapter mentioning sleep. It just nods off the reader and gives them permission to stop reading, put the book down and never pick it up again. I can't have that! As lengthy as this letter is, **it's critical that my readers get to the last page before noon on January 1st.**

I was sitting at the desk in the library of our new home, minding my own business, studying my notes on cliff-hanger chapter endings and other lessons Mary Bargteil had taught me in her Memoir writing course at Anne Arundel Community College when I heard a blood-curdling scream. The scream seemed to be coming from right inside the bookshelves lining the walls of the room. The very same bookshelves that cloaked the entrance to a secret passageway leading to a three-story spiral staircase plunging deep beneath the calm façade of Osprey Point to the reinforced-concrete panic room buried under the foundations.

"What was that?" I wondered aloud as I went to investigate.

Chapter 3

It All Started In Hawaii

"A blood-curdling scream?" Wendy asked. "Did you skip class when Mary taught never to use clichés in your writing?"

"No," I replied sheepishly. "I was there."

"If you don't stop messing around and get going with our holiday greetings, this Christmas Book is dead before it starts. There wasn't any scream—blood-curdling or not. Quit tricking our readers to keep them reading. Either take them to Hawaii or get on to describing our Muddy Boot Open House last January 2nd. Step on it."

"Hawaii briefly, then on to the Muddy Boots party."

"Show, don't tell. Or did you miss that class too?"

* * *

My father was an Army brat. In the 1920s and early 1930s, he and his sister, Thelma, attended High School in Honolulu while my grandfather manned the big coastal artillery guns protecting Pearl Harbor. When my grandfather was rotated back to the mainland, Aunt Thelma decided to stay in Hawaii and become a school teacher. With easy access to mimeograph machines at work, and long distance telephone calls costing a day's pay for a brief conversation, Thelma was an early adopter of the lengthy holiday letter format. The "Chronicles of the Craigs" were eagerly anticipated in our house each December as we caught up with the events in our cousins lives half a world away.

While initially scornful of the idea of form letter greetings, with the advent of the Personal Computer in the early 1980s, my nuclear family followed suit as my mother started putting out the standard two-page report of our successes—glossing over our failures in keeping with the conventional style of the genre.

After our wedding, Wendy and I started putting out our own version of the seasonal diary of major events, but kept distribution limited to avoid driving off our friends in boredom. By Christmas 2000, we had even bored ourselves to tears and were back to just sending cards.

In April of 2001, things changed. I signed up for a five-week course on writing at the college where Wendy works to try and get some guidance on improving my Intracoastal Waterway book for publication. From that course I was introduced to the Maryland Writers' Association, and soon became friends with a group of local writers—all very interesting and creative people.

After a hiatus of a year, Wendy and I reintroduced our Xmas Letter for the 2001 Christmas season. Primarily a writing exercise in the beginning, we still kept distribution small, sending cards to most of our list. I was trying to find my "writer's voice", the rhythm and flow of my prose.

From that point on, each year's letter has been an attempt to top the previous effort. What follows are the unabridged Xmas Letters of Jon & Wendy Coile—2001 to 2005. We hope you enjoy them, but whatever you do, don't forget to get to the last page of this book before noon on January 1st. Now you can go the short way and just flip to the back, but don't you think that is kind of cheating? Just buckle down, get reading and slog your way through our tales of family adventures and you'll be there before you know it. Here goes...

Christmas—2001

Chapter 4

Our 9/11 Experience

Merry Christmas!

It's been two years since we sent our last Holiday Letter. The year 2000 was a strange one for us and as the holiday season rolled around last year we just didn't feel we had enough good news to share, so kept our tales of woe to ourselves.

September 11th, 2001 put things in a different light for the entire country, and our own minor little bumps in the road of life have taken on a newly diminished perspective. We are back to sharing our adventures in a Christmas Letter. (By the way, we always enjoy the ones we receive from friends so keep it up if you are sending one!)

On the fateful 9/11 Wendy was starting the second day of her two weeks of Active Duty as a Commander in the Naval Reserve. She drills in the office of Rear Admiral Jenkins, the Competition Advocate of the Navy for Acquisition Management. The Admiral's office is across the street from the Pentagon in the Crystal City office complex. Wendy was on the phone to another reservist when the airliner impacted the Pentagon.

"There's smoke coming from the Pentagon!" her friend told her.

"There's smoke coming from the Pentagon?" Wendy repeated back, trying to make sense of the incomprehensible. Even being less then a mile away, Wendy hadn't heard the crash and didn't understand at first what was going on. She hung up the phone and went into the Admiral's office where the rest of the staff had gathered to look out the windows at the black smoke billowing from the Pentagon outer ring. They were listening to the news on the radio when suddenly the entire building shook with a sharp boom. A secondary explosion? Another plane crash? The radio news soon announced that it was a sonic boom from fighters arriving over Washington to defend the Capitol from any other inbound aircraft.

Before I go any further, let me go back to the summer of 2000, when another incident with an airplane contributed to our not sending a Christmas letter last year.

Chapter 5

The Aircraft Accident

Every August, the Experimental Aircraft Association has their big fly-in convention in Oshkosh, Wisconsin. This little farm town swarms with 12,000 planes and nearly a million visitors for a week of total aviation ecstasy. Pipers, Cessnas, warbirds, homebuilts, and acres and acres of everything imaginable for the aviation enthusiast. It is the flying equivalent of Woodstock. The biggest aviation gathering on the planet and it happens every summer.

For Oshkosh 2000, my plane partner Mike Baldwin and I loaded up our Piper Seneca with my old buddy Fred, and his brother-in-law Sandy, plus all the camping gear we could carry. We took off for Michigan for a quick enroute fuel stop, and then on to Oshkosh. With all the little airplanes flying in from around the country the field becomes the busiest airport in the world for the week of the show. There are actually more takeoffs and landings per day at Oshkosh Whitman Field then there are at Chicago O'Hare. We joined the packed traffic pattern and dived down for a landing after the organized chaos of the Ripon Approach, infamous in pilot circles.

At the end of the exciting week of aviation immersion, we were ready to load up and fly out at dawn. The weather briefer told us that we could expect the typical mid-west summer weather pattern. Calm but rainy skies in the morning, with thunderstorms starting to build after lunch, and a dangerous pattern of thunderstorms churning up the atmosphere by late afternoon.

We climbed into the plane before 8:00am and called ground control for our clearance, and hit a big snag. Chicago Center was swamped with other IFR traffic. They were holding planes on the ground at Oshkosh so we didn't saturate the Air Traffic Control system. We were number fourteen on the list for an instrument departure and they told us to sit tight and check back in a half hour. The half hour stretched to an hour, then another, then still another hour.

We considered taking off VFR and sneaking out through the light rain showers falling from the low cloud deck. Not a bright idea we all decided, so we waited. While we sat waiting, unbeknownst to us, a four seat plane was inbound for Oshkosh from the west. They were scud running below the clouds, getting pushed closer to the ground by the intermittent rain squalls, trying to drag it in to the field VFR. Less then 20 miles from Oshkosh a large windmill tower leapt out of the mist and clipped their wing, spiraling the Cessna 182 into the ground, killing all four men onboard. At Oshkosh we waited on.

Noon came and went and we were now getting into the Thunderstorm zone. We needed to go now. We got the call to start our engines and we taxied up to the runway. Only two planes in front of us. We waited, props turning. Minutes passed and the first plane was released into the murk. We waited, and the second plane went. We were number one for take off. We finally launched, just before 1:00pm.

We climbed up to eleven thousand feet to cross Lake Michigan and started altering our course to the south to avoid the thunderstorm buildups that were due east. Air Traffic Control was good about trying to help us steer around the thunderstorms, correlating their radar returns with the storm scope data we were getting in the cockpit. Mike was flying on autopilot while I handled the radios and navigation when ALL HELL BROKE LOOSE!

Kablam! The plane went wild, like a car driven off a highway into a rocky drainage ditch. The thunderstorm shoved us upward with an unbelievable force. We shot up through 12,000 feet, then 13,000, and still higher, sucked up into the storm in a massive updraft. The altimeter wound upwards like a cartoon clock gone haywire.

No time to think. Training kicked in as thoughts raced through my consciousness*...no oxygen onboard...we can't go any higher...we've got to stop this climb before we pass out!*

The wings dropped right, and then left, then back to the right, banking at crazy angles approaching 45 degrees each time. Mike punched off the autopilot and struggled with the yoke to hold us level.

"Power back to 25 inches...wings level...get the nose down...don't fight every gust...try and hold attitude...don't let her climb!" I yelled at Mike over the din of rain pummeling our small aluminum aircraft. Lightning lit up the inside of the cloud as bolts shot by horizontally just behind us, as if spanking us to get out of there. We needed no encouraging!

"I've got the plane. Get us out of here!" Mike yelled.

I called on the radio for help from the controllers. "We're in a cell! Give us a steer out of this NOW."

Turn to the right they calmly encouraged from the security of their earthbound radar room. The controller couldn't share our pain as we slammed around the cabin trying to cinch down our seatbelts to keep from bouncing off the roof. He carefully guided us out of the maelstrom. Within a few seconds the ride calmed down to the level of plain old Severe Turbulence. Five minutes later we were through and taking stock of our situation: Plane intact (or so we thought); extremely distraught passengers; and somewhat distraught pilots.

That's not exactly accurate. Mike and I were feeling something akin to the glow you get from a major accomplishment. We knew the bad stuff was behind us. Our passengers, on the other hand, were extremely anxious with the fear for what might happen next. They strongly implored us to get on the ground ASAP.

We called our helpful controller and he diverted us to the nearest big airport: Toledo, Ohio. When we taxied to the ramp and got out we were shocked to find that the plane was badly beaten up. The leading edge of the wing and tail was flailed clean of paint by the torrential rains. The nose, wing tips, tail, and fiberglass fairing components on the plane were dinged, smashed or missing pieces. Shattered plastic and fiberglass greeted us everywhere we looked.

Even though it was only mid-afternoon, we were done flying for the day!

We went to a Holiday Inn with an absolutely awful karaoke bar and drank our dinner with a cacophony of horrendous singing from the "regulars" in the background. Thankful to be alive, we shot pool, drank beer, Monday-morning-quarterbacked the flight countless times, and just enjoyed being alive at the Toledo Holiday Inn.

When I got home, Wendy said she just couldn't imagine me going to Oshkosh and not coming back. I don't think I can imagine that either. Like all pilots, I've been convinced that I'm a safe conscientious pilot. One of the safer ones, actually. I still believe that, but now I have a much higher respect for the elements beyond my control, and the limitations of what my plane and I are capable of. We ended up doing $15,000 damage to the plane in flight, but the insurance picked up most of the repair. We now have a brand new paint job on the entire plane.

After reading this far, you may be asking yourself two things:

1. Why would I ever go flying with this guy? (Trust me. I'm not doing that again.)
2. I thought this was a Christmas Letter. Where's the Baby Jesus? (I almost met him.)

Chapter 6

The Scam Artist

Anyway, life after Oshkosh settled back into the routine. In early October of 2000 I had a business meeting in Seattle, so Wendy came with me and we had a great week running around, seeing the sights, hooking up with old friends, shopping at the original Nordstrom's, and more. A nice vacation, with some business thrown in.

I was checking e-mail before dinner, our last night in Seattle, when I spotted an unusual little message from my dad:

"Jonathan. May I please borrow $75,000 ASAP? Love, your Father."

My parents are in their 70's and 80's, and live in Pacific Grove, California. Typical depression era folks, they have no mortgage, lots of retirement income from saving frugally all their lives, they're actually still working and bringing home a paycheck, and they have ZERO debt. I couldn't imagine how they could possibly need seventy five large. I picked up the phone and dialed home.

"Dad. I got your e-mail and I'm a little confused. What do you need the money for? Are you O.K.?" I asked as soon as he answered.

"We're fine! It's not for us. It's for Whitney." Dad cheerfully replied.

Arrgghh! Whitney! My arch-nemesis! The butt snorkeling little weasel who, with his wife Rita, latched on to my parents more then a decade earlier. Surrogate kids to my folks while all three of us real kids were living 3,000 miles away on the East Coast. Whit & Rita were constantly over at my parent's house ingratiating themselves through small favors. What did he want with the money, I innocently enquired.

Dad is a PhD engineer. He knows an absolute ton about a lot of subjects, but business and law aren't two of them. He tried to explain, "He has a lawsuit on a contract or something and he is going to win a million dollars in the spring. He needs the *$75,000* for a retainer for the lawyer who is taking the case."

I'd heard rumors about this lawsuit for a couple years. Some former partner in a financial planning business who supposedly embezzled all the money from the partnership and disappeared. Whit & Rita had been so distraught they filed bankruptcy and then moved in and mooched off my parents for NINE months; My Sister, Brother and I were starting to think about legal moves to get them out of the folks' house back then, when they left of their own accord. Still, what my father was saying didn't make sense. What kind of lawsuit requires a retainer of *$75,000* up front when you are the Plaintiff? Normally you just sign a contingency agreement with your attorney and pay them a percentage of whatever they are able to get for you in the end. I didn't understand, and Dad wasn't able to help clarify the situation. I said I'd get back to him and rung off.

Wendy and I talked it over, and decided something was fishy. Wendy made me do the right thing as a son, and I cancelled my flight home and caught a plane down to Monterey in the morning. The folks arranged for Whitney to pick me up at the airport.

"Hi, Whit. Thanks for coming to pick me up." I insincerely offered to the tall gangly loser who showed up in his ten year old BMW.

"Rita and I want you to know how much we are indebted to you for loaning us the money." Whitney said.

Keep dreaming, scumbag, I silently thought, as I resisted the strong urge to tear into the details to find out what exactly was going on. We made small talk as Whit drove along the coast road to my parents' house and arrived in a few minutes, just in time for lunch on the patio. My parents had always bragged about Whit's accomplishments like he was their own son. Ivy League like my Dad, Whit had a Masters from Dartmouth and a Business degree from Wharton. He was allegedly a former Naval Officer too, which also appealed to my Navy League Dad. These stories always seemed a little suspect to us real kids.

For one, Whit didn't ever seem to have much of a job for the ten years we knew him as he and Rita hovered around the folks. For a couple years Whit was supposedly the Assistant Manager of the Inn at Spanish Bay in Pebble Beach. When the folks took us all there for lunch during one family visit, we were surprised to find Whit was wearing the same apron as the other bus boys and waiters. Didn't seem to fit with my vision of what most Wharton grads would be doing by age 40.

Second big clue was his Naval Officer story. Supposedly he was a Surface Warfare Officer on the USS Shasta in the early 80's. I was a naval officer myself; in Surface Warfare; in the early 80's, in the same homeport as the Shasta. I knew two of the officers from the Shasta Wardroom pretty well, but Whitney didn't remember them. That's just hard to believe when you work so close together with a group of only 25 officers on the ship. Normally when you get two naval officers together, no matter where or when they served, they start swapping sea stories. No matter how I started the conversation, I could never get Whit to talk about the Navy. That's weird.

After lunch, Dad, Whit and I went in to the living room to go over the case. To cut a very, very, very long story short, Whit outlined his elaborate scheme whereby he created a fictitious company, The Anglo-French Bank Corp., and applied for a disability insurance policy based on earning $200,000 per year as the Vice President. Two years after he got the policy he automatically got under the protections of the incontestability clause of the contract. From that point forward fraud on the application was no longer a legally acceptable reason for the insurance company to decline to pay him benefits. Then, big surprise, he got "sick". The sickness of choice for these fraud-artists is Chronic-Fatigue Syndrome as there is no exact medical test for the insurance company to use to prove you DON'T have it.

As Whit laid out his story, he told us he had done this before in the late 80's and after receiving $10,000 a month for a year, the insurance company gave him a lump sum of $600,000 to buy-out his disability insurance contract. Unfortunately he spent all the money, and even though his wife, Rita, had also done her own disability insurance scam as the "Vice President" of the fictitious Carmel Capital Corp, they blew all the money in four years, filed bankruptcy, moved in with MY parents and started the scam all over again. The first thing he did to start the new scam was to legally change his name from "Whitney Paige Dirtball" to "Miles Cameron Scumbag". The "Dirtball" moniker was already in the insurance company fraud database so he needed to establish a new identity.

As I sat listening in shock, Whit then described the elaborate legal dealings he had been through with the insurance company who were trying to avoid paying him for the current scam. He had dismissed two different lawyers who were "such Boy Scouts," but had finally found some sleaze-bucket lawyer to take the case. This new attorney was demanding an upfront retainer of *$75,000.*

I made some lame excuse about doing a conference call with his new attorney and my attorney on Monday before I gave him the $75,000 and hustled him out of the house. I wanted some time alone with my sister, Jennifer to figure this out. This was going to rock my parents to the core, once they understood what was happening.

Chapter 7

Disgorging the Scamsters

After Whitney drove off, Jennifer and I went for a walk. We had to go back in and tell my parents that despite what they had believed for more then a decade, Whit and Rita were not the good people they believed them to be.

We went back home, gathered in the kitchen with the folks, and Jennifer and I quietly explained the truth. Luckily, Whit had left 140 pages of legal documents for me including the legal brief from the disability insurance company. We showed the folks where the insurance fraud investigator had determined that Whit had never attended Dartmouth or Wharton; that the various executive positions he and his wife held were fictitious, for non-existent corporations; and that they had a pattern of committing insurance fraud over the past decade.

As the light started to come on for my parents, my mother quietly said, "I've loaned Whitney some money."

Oh, great, I thought. What else could there possibly be to this story? It ultimately came out that Whit and Rita had borrowed eighteen thousand dollars over a period of two years, stating small and building to thousands of dollars at a clip. Needless to say, they had never paid back a penny.

Jennifer and I were just recovering from this news that Whit & Rita had "borrowed" thousands when the other shoe dropped. My mother said, "I guess we should take them out of our will now too."

After much effort, we got Whit & Rita out of the will, out of the house, and out of our parents' life. The California Department of Insurance Fraud arrested Whit and put him in jail for several days until he could make bail. He's out now, awaiting trial, and will probably get a three year sentence, suspended unless and until he does this again in

California. The money he got from the folks is long gone, but at least we got our parents back.

So, after the emotional rollercoaster of these two events, we ended 2000 not in much of a mood to tell our tale in a Christmas letter. Time heals all, and after the events of 2001 we are in more of a sharing mood. Since you've hung in this long, we are going to accelerate up to speed and roar through a brief synopsis of this past year, and wrap up with the rest of the "Wendy at the Pentagon" story.

Chapter 8

The Traditional Blah-blah

The end of 2000 saw a few other changes for us. We sold *Griffin*, and closed out that chapter of our boating life. You may remember that *Griffin* was our flybridge powerboat that we cruised from Severna Park to Miami for the winter several years ago. We decided that once was enough, on *Griffin* anyway, and put her up for sale in the summer of 2000. She sold quickly so we were ready to go shopping when Boat Show Season rolled around.

Griffin had two small diesel engines and cruised along at a comfortable 17 knots. There is a time in your life for everything, and this year, for me, it's Speed! *Zest,* our new boat, is 28 feet long. On the water she looks like a floating mini-van. Technically she is a Chaparral 280 SSi bow rider. Seats 12, enclosed head compartment, built-in refrigerator in the cockpit, double bimini top that covers half the boat giving us plenty of space to stretch out away from the sun. She's a great party/family boat. But Under the engine hatch are TWO snarling Mercruiser Magnum MPI fuel injected three hundred horsepower V-8s! Six hundred ponies! And here's the best part: Each engine drives TWO props! We have as many propellers as the Battleship New Jersey! Bravo III outdrives for those interested in the details.

Our biggest problem is not getting suckered in by the temptation to re-calibrate every punk in a go-fast on the Severn River. When somebody comes flying by our bimini covered family truckster in a Cigarette, Formula, or Scarab, I have to restrain the urge to grab the two Gaffrig racing throttles and hammer a little humility into them. Now I'm not the fastest boat on the river by a long shot, but if you pick your fights, you can always win! If somebody really fast comes up astern, I just stay in Mini-Van mode and let them blow on by. But, give me a punk in a 50 mph boat and he's toast as we roar past at 60+, bimini top flapping in the gale force breeze! I think youth might favor a "no-go showboat" but at the ripe old age of 44 I'm having fun with my "sleeper".

In March we were in Jacksonville on our way to Key West when Wendy tore her calf muscle. We were playing a little game of old people volleyball with some friends. Nothing too aggressive. Wendy stepped wrong on the uneven playing field and POW. The healing process was set back severely when she re-injured her calf two months into the healing process. It took therapy all summer, and special stretching exercises morning and night to get it fixed, but she is finally all better. The older we get, the harder it is to heal, but you knew that.

In June we flew to California to see my 8-year-old niece in her first ballet recital. Sienna was one of a cast of thousands, from toddlers up to high school age girls in a massive two-day dance recital in San Francisco. We had a great weekend with the family, enjoying the Bay Area lifestyle at sister-in-law Lori's home in Alameda.

For those of you who know my sister Jennifer, she and husband John, along with daughter Sienna are now living in Hollister, California. John is teaching art at the high school and is back in his element; Jennifer is doing planning work, telecommuting from home; and Sienna can walk the two blocks to school. They are all doing great, settling back into America after five years in the Foreign Service. Plus, they now live only forty miles away from our folks so they can watch out for Whit & Rita types.

My brother Andrew also moved to California with his partner Steve. They live in the L.A. area where Andrew is Vice President of a dotcom. The dotcom part has given them a fairly exciting ride, but they like the weather.

In the summer of 2001 I decided to give Oshkosh a miss for the first time since 1994. Instead we went to the Thousand Islands of upstate New York. Wendy's family has a place up there in Clayton, NY, so a whole bunch of her peeps descended on the "camp" for a week in August. Our contribution to the party was a king size white sheet, DVD player, and the loan of the 1100 lumen LCD projector from the office. Every night, after sunset, we fired up the projector, popped in a DVD disk and watched a movie that filled the entire sheet, hung on the wall of the living room. It was bigger, closer, and brighter then the best Movie Theater with Stadium Seating. Like our own little IMAX theater! It was a great week overall, and the movies were just the icing on the cake.

In September Wendy and I celebrated our fourteenth wedding anniversary, and in October it was the BIG birthday for Wendy. You can guess the number. Or not.

In early November, I was on a business trip when my cell phone rang. I looked at the little caller ID window on my phone. It was Mike, my plane partner. I hit the send button to take the call.

"Hi, Mike. How are you?"

"Hi, Jon. I've had a little problem with the plane. I taxied the left wheel into a ditch and the prop hit the ground." Mike said. He went on to describe how the prop tips barely hit and only bent back the last two inches of each blade. The prop strike was so soft that the engine didn't stop, just quietly chewed away at the edge of the taxiway until Mike could shut it down. It doesn't really make much difference. Once the prop hits the ground, the engine has to come off the plane and get torn down for a complete inspection.

No problem I told Mike. The important thing was nobody was hurt. Just a little bit of time and money and we will be better then new. Our airplane insurance company has our pictures up on their dartboard at this point after buying us a paint job and an engine. As you read this, the new engine is being installed, then the new prop will go on and we'll be back in business by Christmas, we hope.

I wouldn't have mentioned Mike's prop strike, and probably kept the secret of our little Oshkosh Thunderstorm Adventure, if I hadn't bumped into Jim Hunter. I hardly know Jim, having only met him once. He's one of the people in the real estate industry that straddles the fence between the real estate brokerage side where I am, and the homebuilder side where Mike makes his living. In a casual meeting, Jim popped out, "Oh. I bumped into Mike Baldwin at a homebuilder's meeting last week. He told me he wrecked your plane."

Well now, I figure if Mike is going to tell casual strangers about his prop strike then maybe I should lighten up and come clean on our Oshkosh adventure.

We had planned to fly to Key West for Thanksgiving this year, but with the prop bent we drove to Wendy's sisters' in upstate New York instead. We are heading to California for a Coile Christmas and to celebrate my parent's 50th wedding anniversary before we head home to close out 2001.

Back to 9/11. I was in a meeting at the office when someone came in and told us that a plane had hit the Pentagon. I immediately ran outside and tried to call Wendy's cell phone from mine. "All circuits are busy." I tried several times and just couldn't get an open line. I ran back to my office and tried to call from my desk. No joy. I fished out Wendy's direct dial number at the Admirals' office and tried again. "All circuits are busy." I kept dialing, trying both her numbers. Cell, desk, cell, desk, cell, desk. Finally, after the longest half hour of my life we got through to each other.

The Admiral went ahead and cut loose the staff to get out of town and head for home. In the uncertainty that prevailed during the morning of 9/11 they were not alone. The entire working population of Washington was trying to egress back to the suburbs. A normal one-hour commute stretched to five hours as the traffic snarl crept down Route One away from the city. Pedestrians walking on the road passed the cars trapped in traffic as jet fighters roared low overhead, guarding the city. For the first hour Wendy's rear view mirror was filled with the reflection of tragedy as the pillar of black smoke rose from the Pentagon.

Like many in the United States, we have a renewed belief in God and Country since 9/11, and we'll leave it at that. We wish you and yours a happy, safe, fulfilling 2002.

Merry Christmas and a Happy New Year!

P.S. I forgot to mention that I joined the Maryland Writers' Association this year. They've put me on the Board of Directors, made me the co-Coordinator of the annual 250 person Writer's Conference, and I'm also in a critique group that meets twice a month. As you might have guessed from this letter I'm enjoying my new hobby immensely. Holy, molly, I just checked the word processor stats. This Christmas Letter is almost 5,000 words! I think I got a little carried away this time. Next year I'll try and make it a short story.

Christmas—2002

Teaching the Diary of
CAUTION

CAUTION

Enclosed is the unauthorized Jon & Wendy Coile Christmas Letter 2002.

I gave my husband permission to write a brief, light-hearted, two-page holiday letter to send to our family and friends.

What he produced was a 32-page mini-magnum opus, filled with swearing, fighting drunks, professional wrestling, soap opera stars, international immigration scams and who knows what else he's made up.

Even if he apparently doesn't, I do know how busy people are at the holidays, and that you probably don't have time to read long rambling letter like this. Please accept my apologies and feel free to throw this away without reading.

Merry Christmas.

Wendy Coile

Chapter 9

Sparring with "Richard Head"

"...five, four, three, two, one, Happy New Year 2002!"

Wendy and I kissed as Dick Clark droned on in the background, fireworks exploding on the tiny TV screen at the foot of the bed. Unlike my literary friends, I wasn't sharp enough to pick up on the fact that these fireworks might be a metaphor for the year ahead.

* * *

January 1st, 2002 was a beautiful winter day in Maryland. Mild by our terms, with a weak sun lifting the temperature into the low 40's. I went down to the pier in the backyard to finish prepping our boat in the lift to withstand the snows of winter. After a pleasant hour just messing about, I climbed off *Zest* and started walking up the pier back to the house. Out of the corner of my eye I noticed a man crabbing across my neighbor's yard, trying to maneuver into position to intercept me at the shoreline. I didn't recognize the stranger but he looked angry. About my age, a few inches taller and tough, as if he worked in a trade where he lifted heavy objects, or maybe just pumped iron with his prison buddies. A sharp scowl added definition to his chiseled features.

"ARE YOU JON COILE?" he barked.

"Yes," I replied.

"WELL I'M RICHARD HEAD!" (Not his actual name. More of an honorific.) "I WANT YOU TO SEE MY FACE SO YOU'LL RECOGNIZE ME. I'M GOING TO <bleep> YOU OVER! I'M GOING TO REDUCE YOUR <bleep>ING HOUSE TO MATCHSTICKS. I'M GOING TO <bleep> WITH YOU FOR THE NEXT 25 <bleep>ING YEARS, YOU <bleep>, <bleep>, <bleep>, <bleep>, <bleeeeeeeeep>!"

Who IS this guy, I thought, as my professional training kicked into gear instinctively. No. Not my military training. Real estate.

One of the interesting aspects of my job at Champion Realty is that I am the last stop for customer complaint calls. We have great agents on the front lines, and experienced, tactful managers soothing ruffled feathers every day, so it doesn't happen very often, but when you sell 4,000 homes a year, occasionally you run into an unbelievably irate person. When there is no calming them down at the branch office level, the call gets routed to me. Over the years I have developed my 37-minute theory of hostile behavior. When I get a hostile call I pull out a pad to take notes, set my timer for 37 minutes, and ask them to tell me about the problem.

It's like clockwork. The person rants and raves in ever decreasing waves of drama, and in 37 minutes they calm back down to normal levels of human communication. My theory goes that it's not possible to maintain an hysterical level of anger for more than 37 minutes in the face of a calm, reasonable person who doesn't argue back. The second part of my theory, based on experimental data, is that there is no way to short-circuit this anger reduction process. They need to unload and be heard until the steam has totally dissipated. When confronted by a lunatic at work, I just clear my schedule for 37 minutes and ride it out.

I observed the lunatic ranting in front of me. His cheeks were flushed, spittle flying from the corners of his mouth, and a small vein bulging from his temple. His eyes glared, filled with fire, while his jaw chomped up and down as if he was chewing the words he screamed at me. *So this is what they look like on the other end of the phone.*

As the tirade ramped up to full bore I measured angles and distances with my eyes, confirming that I had zero chance of outrunning him if I bolted. For one, he had the advantage of the high ground, standing up on my raised brick patio, three steps up from my position on the grass lawn. Second, there was no doubt about who was in better shape. He had the six-pack-abs thing going while I look as if I swallowed the keg.

As he yelled obscenities at me I stepped in towards him to close the distance. I wasn't suicidal, just trying to stay in his comfort zone. Close enough so he would know I was paying attention, but not so close that he could take a swing without me getting a step or two of advance warning, for whatever that was worth.

He continued with, "You <bleep>ing <bleep>. You've been <bleep>ing with my family for years. <bleep>,<bleep>."

Is he mental? I'd met his Dad casually only once, for maybe three minutes, seven years ago. I don't think I could pick any of the Head family out of a line-up if my life depended on it, so how could I have been <bleep>ing with them? I noticed that while he still ranted, the tempest was slowly starting to subside. A quick glance at my watch showed that he was almost done. As I listened, I realized what his problem was.

Basically the issue is that this clown's father has a property line dispute with a neighbor and thanks to one incorrectly annotated plat from his incompetent engineer in 1995, the whole family was apparently convinced that I was the source of the possible encroachment. The minor fact that he had to walk around a 3,600 square foot home to get to my property didn't seem to register in his pea brain. He just knew he wanted to kick my ass, and I equally knew that I did not want to get the snot smacked out of me at 44 years of age. I had really hoped that stuff was behind me as I entered my teens.

"Richard," I started, when the outburst had slowed to a crawl. "Can I call you Dick?"

He glared, nostrils flaring slightly. I could see the gears grinding as he struggled to come up with a snappy retort.

"Never mind," I continued, cutting to the chase. "See those two piers?" I pointed to the water between his Dad's pier and my own. "There are actually two property owners between your Dad and me. It's a mistake on a plat from seven years ago. I don't have any contiguous property lines with your family. It's physically impossible for me to encroach on your lot."

He looked around, as if he was seeing the landscape for the first time. As he twirled slowly, he caught sight of the frickin' huge waterfront mansion blocking the view of his Dad's house from my property. His head lolled back as his eyes traveled up the three stories of Pella windows to the hip roof high over our heads. His gaping mouth and stupefied expression confirmed that he hadn't thought this all the way through before coming to see me. He had been, just like his Dad, overreacting to bad information.

His head fell back down to the horizon, mouth shutting with a faint whump as the last shot of steam went out of him.

"<bleep> you," he said, turning his back on me, and with that parting witticism he trudged off.

And just for the record, his whole family is full of <bleep> on the encroachment issue...

* * *

"Stop the presses!" Wendy interrupted me at the computer. "This is a Christmas letter. Where's the Baby Jesus stuff? What kind of stories are you making up now?"

Chapter 10

Skiing with "Captain Morgan"

My loving wife has been patiently tolerating my new hobby—writing—but she is strongly encouraging me to get back to the real purpose of this letter: to tell our family and friends, scattered all over the world, about the major events that have happened in our lives in 2002. I'll try hard to keep to the facts, but this letter is just so much more fun for me to write if I "enhance" the story slightly. All the events in here are based on the truth, but so I don't become the first person ever sued for their Christmas Letter, I am now going to say that it's all fiction. Any resemblance to persons living or dead, and especially if you think you are one of the ignorant jerks portrayed in any incident described in these pages, is purely coincidental. Now that the legal disclaimer business is over, back to the story. Let's see, in the time line we were up to 2:00 p.m. on January 1st.

* * *

After such a rocky start to the year, it seemed like things could only get better. We flew to Key West with our airplane partners, Mike and Gina Baldwin, for a long week-end in mid-January and had a great time. The highlight of the trip was a ride in a turbo-prop Cessna Caravan on amphibious floats out to Fort Jefferson for a day of sightseeing and snorkeling. Mike and I weaseled our way up into the cockpit, each getting a turn in the right seat for a first-hand view of seaplane operations. This planted the seed for something that happened in the summer, but I shouldn't get ahead of myself here.

* * *

Coming off the pleasant week-end in Key West, when February came around we were very excited to head out west to Montana for our first ever ski trip to the Rocky Mountains.

Wendy has a friend who recently re-married. Over the past few years we had gotten into the habit of going out to dinner every few months with the new couple. Lucy and Ricky Cranium (not their actual names) were easy dinner companions, so we stepped up to taking a week-long vacation with them in 1999. The week we spent on a dive boat cruising off the west coast of the big island of Hawaii, was pleasant and uneventful, probably due more to the five-person crew taking care of eight divers, then anything the Craniums did, or didn't do. Anyway, when Lucy called Wendy and suggested we rent a condo at Big Sky, Montana for a week, it sounded like fun, even though we are not very good skiers.

Lucy and Ricky's friends, Chuck and Judy, also signed on for the trip. We planned to fly into Salt Lake City, during the height of the Olympics, and change planes for Bozeman. Mingling with the arriving athletes at the airport in Salt Lake made us feel a small part of the Olympic excitement. When we got to Bozeman our luggage and skis for six adults absolutely packed the rented minivan to the rafters and we still needed to buy groceries. After lunch in town, we headed to a wholesale club for boxes and boxes of provisions, and then to a liquor store for beer and wine. Ricky added a couple bottles of Capt. Morgan rum to the pile and we all wedged ourselves back into the van, with Wendy and me literally buried at the very back of the van. From our seats in the rear we couldn't see what Ricky was up to in the driver's seat, as he laced his Diet Coke with Capt. Morgan rum for the drive to Big Sky.

As we wound up the mountain road, climbing up from the valley floor towards our mountain condo over 7,500 feet above sea level, Ricky kept swigging at his rum. The black winding road led through a picturesque river gorge, and as the sun set behind the tall ridge to our west, the pitch black darkness of night came quickly to the deep valleys of the Rockies. In the headlights we could see snow covering the sharp crags on our left, and caught an occasional glimpse of boulders in the river beyond the thin galvanized guard-rail to our right. Ricky sipped on.

Our first indication that something was amiss was when we pulled into the snow covered driveway of our condo and exited the van.

"Come-on Chuck," Ricky slurred as he dove at Chuck, shoving him off his feet and into the snow bank next to the driveway. "I want a piece of you. I'm going to kick your butt!"

"Get off of me, you drunken idiot," Chuck pushed Ricky away and got back to his feet, brushing the snow from his parka.

You could have driven a truck into Wendy's mouth as she stared incredulously at the 58-year-old Ricky.

"Come-on Chucky," Ricky whined. "I can take you."

Both Chuck and Ricky topped six feet and 250 pounds, mainly muscle in both their cases, but I was putting my money on a sober Chuck. I tried hard to ignore Ricky and focused on unloading the van, trying to stay out of the mêlée. Apparently when Ricky and Chuck checked in and got the condo keys, Ricky wanted to get the bell-boys from the lodge to come down the mountain the half-mile to our condo to unload the minivan for us. Chuck over-rode that decision, feeling that was an unnecessary waste of our money and more importantly that the bell-boys weren't really dressed to do this, not normally leaving the heated lodge in the performance of their duties. But, as we were all finding out, Ricky didn't like being challenged in his self-anointed leadership role.

Ricky lunged at Chuck as he came out of the condo for another load, slipping at the last second, missing his target. Chuck sidestepped him as he careened into the snow, and continued with the unloading. I thought about tripping on the icy steps and dropping the Capt. Morgan—accidentally of course. To be honest, if I knew how the rest of the week was going to progress I would have done it.

* * *

"What are you doing?" Wendy interrupted me again. "This is a *family* Christmas letter. First bleeps and swear words, now drunks fighting in the snow. What are you thinking? You get back on track or we are sending pictures of Keesha and the cats this year."

"Yes Ma'am," I replied to my wife, Commander, USNR.

Chapter 11

Big Trouble in Big Sky Country

Big Sky is a beautiful resort, nestled high in the Rockies. It was originally developed by Chet Huntley, a fixture at our dinner table in my youth when he co-hosted the Huntley-Brinkley Report on NBC Television in the 60's. Big Sky was his place to relax from anchoring the evening news. In addition to an elegant lodge, the base of the ski slopes is ringed with condos. Our three bedroom, three bath unit had a heated garage for the mini-van, and a 50 yard walk took us to the bottom of a short pommel lift. After getting dragged up the mountain a few hundred yards by the pommel, we were in position to traverse down to the base of the main lifts. Big Sky has cable cars, high-speed quads, and excess capacity to get skiers up the mountain that would be unheard of on the east coast. We never waited for more than four minutes to get on a lift.

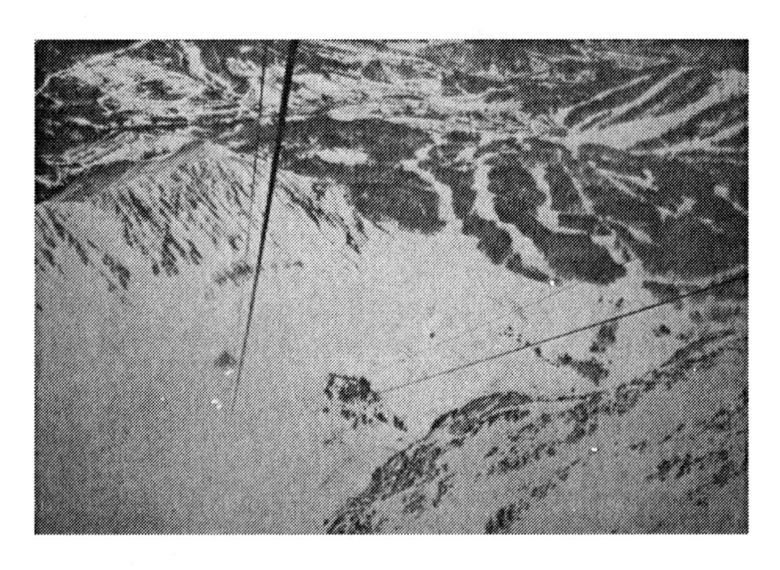

Out on the slopes, the snow conditions were great. Overnight nearly a foot of virgin snow had fallen, blanketing the mountain with fresh powder. Naively we thought we would be in hog heaven—Fresh Powder in the Rockies. Yee-haa!

Wendy and I started slowly, trying to get our skiing skills back up to at least the survival level. The fresh powder snow looked beautiful, unmarred by ski tracks. It was an experienced skier's dream but at our competence level, it was a nightmare. The others went off to attack the mountain on their own, while Wendy and I struggled with the challenge of skiing in the deep snow, our confidence growing as the day wore on.

About 3:00 pm we stopped halfway down the mountain for a brief rest.

"Let's do one more run after this and call it a day," I said.

"No," Wendy replied. "Let's quit now. Most injuries happen on the last run of the day and we've got five more days of skiing ahead of us. We don't need to get it all in today."

"Good point. Let's get going. I'll follow you."

I've been injured three times while skiing. Once in mid-afternoon and twice on the last run of the day. It's probably the combination of your confidence peaking at the same time your muscles are at their most tired state. Your brain knowing how to attack the mountain commands your muscles to move, driving your legs up and down over moguls and bumps. Then suddenly, you hit a bump and one, or both, legs are just too tired to comply. In a split second, realization floods your brain that this isn't going to be a gentle fall like the ones earlier in the day. A leg is being dragged into an unnatural position and too late, you comprehend the strength you possessed before to recover has been sapped by the day's exertions. The sharp pain of ligaments stretched to their breaking point—and beyond—overpowers all thought. After that, there's nothing left but the Ski Patrol sled ride down the mountain, painful surgery, and six months of physical therapy.

We skied down to the bottom, without mishap, and went into the cold, empty condo. I started a fire in the stone fireplace while Wendy prepared some appetizers and drinks. We were relaxing on the sofa, enjoying the tranquility when Chuck burst in the front door.

"Where are the keys to the minivan?" he asked, out of breath, flinging things around in the kitchen in his haste.

"In the bowl on the counter," I replied. "What's the matter?"

"Judy fell. They're bringing her down the mountain in the Ski Patrol sled. I've got to get over to the lodge to take her to the hospital in the van. They think she tore her ACL."

And they were right. Judy's ski trip ended on the first day. At least the skiing part, anyway. That night, since we were trapped in the condo with an injured Judy, Ricky volunteered to cook dinner. Lamb chops broiled in the oven.

Wendy and I were upstairs in our bedroom when the call for dinner came. Opening our bedroom door to the landing, which overlooks the living-dining-kitchen area, acrid smoke stung our eyes.

"What's all that smoke?" Wendy asked.

"Oh, the grease from the lamb chops caught on fire in the oven," replied Lucy. "Ricky put it out."

We came down the stairs to the main level to help set the table for dinner. The smoke was thick throughout the living room, a greasy burnt animal odor that obnoxiously clung to our clothes.

"I'm going to do something about this smoke," I helpfully offered, opening the door to the deck and turning the thermostats to high to change out the air in the condo without freezing our butts off. The pervasive smoke hung in the still air, so I opened the front door to get some cross ventilation as Ricky announced we were ready to eat.

We all sat down at the dinner table to enjoy our plates of burnt lamb chops. The smoke was still stinging our eyes, when suddenly Ricky jumped up and without a word closed all the doors I had opened. I looked around at the smoke, a blue haze still obscuring our view of the room. It wasn't worth fighting over, but I didn't want to live in a greasy smoke condo for the rest of the week. With a cheerful comment, "Let me do something about this smoke," I hopped back up and opened all the doors as if Ricky hadn't just closed them.

"Good idea," said Judy, giving me license to do the appropriate thing.

With a little snort, Ricky stuck his head down and dug into his lamb chops like it was his last meal, ignoring us all. He cut all the meat off the bones, slicing it up and wolfing it down. When he'd achieved all he could with knife and fork, he picked up the remains with his bare hands, and started gnawing the burnt gristle from the bone, not stopping until they were polished clean as a sun-bleached carcass in the desert.

With the smoke cleared I closed the doors, helped clean up the dinner mess, and we retired for the night.

The next night, after a pleasant day of skiing, we decided to go out to dinner eight miles away, at the bottom of the mountain. Buck's T-4 is an internationally known restaurant so we were looking forward to a good meal. Wendy volunteered to be the designated driver so we wouldn't have to worry about Capt. Morgan driving us off a cliff on the way home. Judy hobbled through the restaurant on her crutches and we sat down.

Wendy doesn't like to eat a big meal late at night and then try and go to sleep on a full stomach, so she decided to have a Caesar salad with her club soda. The rest of us dined on Bison tenderloin, Rocky Mountain Trout, and Elk. Chuck, Judy and I shared an inexpensive bottle of wine at our end of the table, while Lucy and Ricky had a $75 bottle of Cabernet Sauvignon.

When the bill came, I noticed that Buck's T-4 may be in the middle of nowhere but they have the latest in hospitality computer information systems.

"Hey, look," I said. "They have the bill itemized by each person's place. It shows that Chuck ordered a Great Plains Bison Tenderloin for $32.50 and a $23 bottle of wine. Isn't that cool."

New technology always gets me excited. I noticed, but didn't mention, that Wendy's place had an itemized bill of $6.50 for the Caesar salad, and $1.50 for the club soda.

"Naw, forget that," said Ricky. "Let's just split the bill three ways. $110 each should do it."

Two days later, Wendy and I having grown slightly weary of skiing, decided to head down the road an hour to Yellowstone National Park for a snowmobile ride in to see Old Faithful in the winter. Lucy and Ricky, hearing of our plans, decided to join us. We all piled in the van, for the drive to Yellowstone, Ricky driving with Lucy up front. As we drove down the mountain, Ricky was making us nervous by looking out the side windows, trying to draw our attention to the various mountain views, as we cruised perilously close to the guard rail protecting us from a plunge down a thousand foot vertical embankment. Lucy could sense our discomfort as we gripped the seat arms and tensed whenever Ricky showboated for just a bit too long resulting in a swerve back off the shoulder and onto the road.

"Ricky, Honey," Lucy said. "Stay on the road now, Sweetums."

"O.K. Honey-Bunny," Ricky replied as he swerved yet again.

It was only an eight-mile ride to the valley floor, but it felt like an eternity. Once down on the bottom, we turned and headed south towards the park. Montana has almost the same population as Anne Arundel County yet it is bigger in total area than the ten North-East states from Maryland to Maine, combined. This sparse population translates into virtually no traffic on the roads outside of the main towns and cities.

We were driving down a two-lane blacktop highway with nary a car in sight when we came upon a small sedan heading our same direction. He was driving fast on the icy surface so there didn't seem to be any need to pass. Ricky pulled right up on his bumper and cruised along, tailgating the only traffic within, literally, five miles in either direction.

As the road took a sharp bend, Ricky stomped on the brakes to avoid the slowing vehicle ahead, opening the distance between the two cars.

"Ricky," I said. "Could you ease back a little bit. You're making us nervous back here."

"If that's what you want, Jon." He replied, sulking from the mild rebuke.

I was getting close to the point of not caring if I insulted him. I wasn't willing to let him risk our lives for some macho insanity on his part. He seemed to be maturely handling my request, but that maturity was short lived.

Within five minutes he was right back up on the bumper of the car ahead, stabbing on the brakes and the accelerator alternately. Lucy was starting to ride him to back off for our sake, when the car in front suddenly slowed to turn into their driveway.

Ricky overreacted, yanking the wheel hard to the left to avoid the rapidly approaching rear corner of the car ahead. Mashing on the brakes, he sent our minivan into a skid at 60 miles an hour. We were sliding sideways down the icy black road as we crossed the centerline into the northbound lane.

Luck came to our rescue that morning as thankfully there was no oncoming traffic to careen into. Ricky recovered from the skid and got us pointed in the right direction, and back in our own lane. You could have heard a pin-drop in the van.

We cruised in silence the rest of the way to the snowmobile rental place and after checking in, I feigned I'd left something in the van and needed the car keys. As I walked back in from the van, I zipped the keys into an inside pocket of my parka and vowed never again to be under this man's control.

* * *

"Can't you write about something nice?" Wendy asked. "All these stories are filled with horrible people and bad events. Can't you tell them about some of the good stuff we did this year?"

"I can do that." I replied.

"Yeah, and make it quicker too. These people have Christmas cookies to bake, and other things to do than listen to your rambling hyperbole. Chop, chop."

"Aye, aye, Ma'am."

Chapter 12

Hobnobbing With the 2nd Richest Man in the World

In April the Maryland Writers' Association held their annual conference just south of Baltimore. This was my second conference to attend and I volunteered to be the conference co-coordinator for the event. Working with an enthusiastic and extremely bright group of 15 people was a very rewarding experience for me. The conference set new attendance records with over 260 people on-site, including agents and editors from New York, former Baltimore Mayor Kurt Schmoke to present the annual writing awards, and more than 30 speakers. Lots of work, by a lot of people, resulted in a very successful event.

* * *

In mid-May, I had the unique experience of being invited to Omaha, Nebraska to have dinner with Warren Buffett, Number 2 on the Forbes list of World's Richest People, and an icon of American business. Our group of real estate companies has hooked up with an energy utility that Buffett's Berkshire Hathaway Company owns, and he invited the management team of our group to come out and have dinner in the private dining room at the top of his office building.

There were 23 of us who were going to get to meet Mr. Buffett. The plan, known in advance for about two months, was for us to mingle in small groups of four, while our HomeServices CEO, Ron Peltier, ushered W.B. around to each group for 90 seconds of "face time" each. Then he would address us as a whole, about our company and how we fit in with his overall business strategy.

Warren Buffett is probably one of the most admired men in business. Unlike some, he has made his huge wealth by ignoring trends and following his own advice. For example, he didn't jump into technology, preferring boring businesses that make money the old fashioned way—with hard work.

The chance to talk to Warren Buffett, one-on-one, didn't have me feeling as anxious as a schoolgirl waiting to get picked up for her Senior Prom, but I *had* been planning my question. I thought everybody was going to ask him about business, or maybe search for common ground and people they may have known in common. My question was going to be unique, at least I hopped it might be.

We were all standing around in our business uniforms. Wendy had bought me a new silk tie, to go with my best "Captains of Industry" suit. We were mingling on station, waiting, when Warren Buffett walked into the room. He may be 72 but when he marches into a room, you can sense the energy. Wearing an inexpensive-looking blue blazer, gray Sansabelt™ slacks, and a polyester tie decorated with small American flags, he wouldn't have been your first guess in the room as to who's the multi-Billionaire.

From left to right: Greg Abel, Warren Buffett, Ron Peltier, Jon's balding head, Chris Coile, Jerry Reece.

"Mr. Buffett," said Ron Peltier. "I'd like you to meet Chris and Jon Coile from Maryland Jerry Reece from Kansas City, and you already know Greg Abel from Mid-American Energy."

"Nice to meet you," said the great man. "Maryland. I used to own a department store in Columbia. Is that near you?"

This one was for Chris. Mr. Buffett and Chris talked about the department store, long closed, and what had happened in the neighborhood in the 30 years since Berkshire got out of discount department stores in Maryland.

It was Jerry Reece's turn. "Yak, yak, yak." I paid scant attention, as I got ready to say my own question, practiced about 200 times for this very occasion.

The spot light turned to me, and with a nod, Ron Peltier gave me my cue.

"Mr. Buffett," I began. "When I told my wife I was going to get to meet you she said, 'Warren Buffett. He's famous.'" I paused a mini-beat to let the obvious sink in, and then continued with Wendy's line. "'He was on *All My Children* with Erica!'"

Mr. Buffett laughed at the memory. "How did that happen?" I continued. "Were you part of the storyline with Adam and Chandler Enterprises or was it Erica and Enchantment, the cosmetics company." I wanted Mr. Buffett to know I had at least a passing knowledge of the soap opera on which he starred.

"Well, I was actually on three episodes. On one I came in to advise Erica on taking Enchantment public, doing an IPO back when they were the rage. On the other two I was the love interest for Opal, the trailer park maven with the bouffant hairdo."

He described the three episodes, and what it was like to film in New York where they produce the soap opera, and then he said, "You know. Something interesting just happened. I was doing my taxes last month and there was a four dollar income item I didn't recognize. I dug into the paperwork and it turns out it was for residuals from the Soap Net Channel for those three episodes. I guess they are still showing them on cable TV."

Ron ushered Mr. Buffett on to the next group of people, while we rehashed every word that had been uttered, looking for pearls of wisdom.

Jerry Reece, CEO of Reece & Nichols, a 4 billion dollar real estate company in Kansas City said, "You know what is the most interesting thing he said? It's that he does his own taxes, and he questions $4 items."

And that, my friends, is probably why he is the second richest man on the planet, and if tech stocks continue on their current course, he'll be back in number one ahead of Bill Gates before you know it.

* * *

"I hate the way you tell that story." Wendy said over my shoulder, looking at the computer screen. "It makes me sound like an idiot. Like I don't know who Warren Buffett is and all I do is watch soap operas."

"Yeah, I know, but it was the only way I could think of to lead into the Erica connection when I met Warren Buffett. I couldn't say *I* watched *All My Children.*"

"All right. But now you need to start thinking about wrapping this up. It's getting way too long."

"But I haven't even mentioned Africa or professional wrestling yet."

"Why don't you use bullets."

"It they don't want to read, they don't have to read it. I'm almost done. Just two more main stories and a couple of anecdotes."

"I'm giving you *Reader's Digest* for Christmas so you can learn how to write more concisely."

"Yeah, yeah," I said turning back to the computer.

Chapter 13

Jell-O® Boy Vs. The Hitman

After the visit to the lair of Warren Buffett, I boarded the plane in Omaha for a flight to Minneapolis. Changing planes for the leg home to Baltimore, I tried to play my trump card at the ticket counter.

Way back in the hey-day of DotComs, in the spring of 2000, I spent three months as a road warrior flying hither and yon, researching "e-mortgage" opportunities for our company. The sole legacy of that era was that I flew so much in such a short period of time, Northwest airlines thinks I might be a good customer in the future. So, if the plane isn't too full, they bump me up into first class for free, to try and entice me to stay loyal and fly a lot more with them.

"Any chance of getting up front," I asked the gate agent. She pulled up my record and compared it to the seating chart.

"Not looking good," she replied, "but if you want to wait here, we'll know in about five minutes."

I was feeling lucky, so I waited.

Looking out toward the terminal, I spotted this huge mesomorph walking directly toward me. Built like an upside-down pyramid, barrel chest and massive biceps topping a ripped abdomen, tight waist, perched on massive thighs, and powerful legs, he was an amazing specimen of the body building art. A ball cap covered his pony tail, a gray sweatshirt emblazoned with "Hitman Hockey" stretched to the breaking point by his muscular chest. He looked intimidating as all hell. Just as he stepped up to the counter, the gate agent turned to me.

"O.K. You're in," she said, as she handed me my boarding card. I bolted for the airplane as she turned her attention to the Hitman.

I sat down in the last row of first class, in the window seat. The flight attendant collected my suit jacket and brought me a glass of Merlot while they finished boarding the plane and prepared for departure. The last man to get on the plane was the mesomorph from the gate, and as he slid into the seat next to me I instinctively eased over towards the window, giving this tough character all the room he wanted.

We took off and within minutes they were serving us dinner on white linen. The mesomorph and I ate in silence, both part of two alien worlds, with seemingly no common ground between us.

After dinner was cleared away, I pulled out a book to read, and happened to glance over at the mesomorph's tray table. He was pulling out a sheaf of papers, done up at the top with a big black binder clip. The text was double spaced and looked suspiciously like a manuscript. I couldn't help myself.

"Are you a writer?" I asked.

"Yes," he replied.

"Really! I am too. What are you writing about?"

"I was a professional wrestler for 23 years. I'm writing about my experiences. How about you?"

"I took a cruise down the Intracoastal Waterway from Annapolis to Miami with my 81-year-old father on a powerboat. It's about how to cruise the waterway, and also about the changing roles between a father and his adult children as we all age."

"Sounds interesting. My dad was a big part of my wrestling career. He used to wrestle himself, and was the person who really got wresting out of the logging camps and on the path to respectability as a sport."

We chatted on, and I asked him his name. If he was Hulk Hogan or The Rock, I might have recognized him, but Professional Wrestling isn't something I normally watch. Turns out I was sitting next to Bret Hart. The "Hitman." Seven time World Champion. Star of both the WWF, and WCW. He was the only professional wrestler to ever appear on the Simpsons cartoon show. You may remember hearing of his brother, Owen Hart. Owen was the wrestler tragically killed in a fall from the top of the arena in Kansas City in 1999 when the cable he was supposed to use to descend into the ring became unclipped. Bret retired recently from wrestling after getting multiple concussions from a mule kick in the back of the head at the MCI center in Washington, D.C. He was on the airplane flying back to D.C. to attend a worker's comp hearing on the mule kick incident the following morning.

As we flew towards Baltimore he captivated me with stories about the world of professional wrestling, from the inside. The drugs: not recreational, or even pain killers, as I might have suspected, but sleeping pills to quiet your body down after the adrenalin of wrestling late into the evening, and then uppers to wake up in the morning for a 6:00 a.m. flight on to the next city on the wresting circuit. It was a grueling schedule. Two shows every Christmas Day for the people who didn't have family to share the holidays with and came out to see wrestling instead. We shared dreams of publishing our books, and as he opened up, I felt I could ask him the big question.

"All right, Bret, I guess we know it's staged, but how exactly is it choreographed? Do they tell you what to do every minute you are wrestling in the ring?"

"Well," he said with a gentle slap to the back of my forearm with his hand, "let's say you and I were going in the ring tonight."

I must have been tired, or maybe it was the Merlot, but my mind wandered off. I was envisioning being in the ring at the MCI center, a sea of faces filling the seats in every direction beyond the ropes. I could hear the announcer's tinny voice as he announced the bout in the hyper-speech used by all fight promoters.

"TONIGHT, IN THE MAIN EVENT, IT'S SEVEN TIME HEAVY-WEIGHT CHAMPION OF THE WORLD, BRET "HITMAN" HART VERSUS, THE CHALLENGER, IN THE LEMON YELLOW TIGHTS AND SHERBERT ORANGE CAPE, NEWCOMER, JON "JELL-O® BOY" COILE."

I was looking down, admiring the taxi-cab yellow body stocking, wide white belt and boots, and the orange cape dangling down my back, when I felt myself being lifted high over the mat. Hitman spun me around a couple times, the sea of faces blurring as they raced past and then I felt myself flying, weightless, the ropes passing beneath me as I soared out of the ring. The unoccupied plastic folding chairs coming up at me looked like a reasonably soft landing spot, as I came crashing down...

"...before we go into the ring, we'd sit down in the locker room and have a cup of coffee. The promoter would tell us how they wanted the fight to end. Maybe even tell us what to do in the last two minutes. Then you and I would talk through the rest of the fifteen-minute bout. We wouldn't script out every second, but we'd have an idea how it was going to play out. It's really an art form to be able to jump down from the top of the ropes and land on somebody's chest with your knee and not hurt them. A few inches either way and you can cause serious damage."

As we pulled into the gate at Baltimore, I asked him my final question. Many of his stories had been the heartache he had endured pursuing the wrestling career. The ongoing problems from his concussions, the strain that broke up his marriage, never being home for Christmas with his kids, the loss of his brother Owen, and other incidents in his career that had been unpleasant experiences, many dealing with the promoters of the sport.

"So," I asked. "Would you do it again?"

"Well," Bret paused for reflection. "I wish I could have my brother back, but other than that, it's been a good life."

We got off the plane and said goodbye in the terminal. He left me with the impression that he is a gentle, decent man, and I wish him the best of luck getting his book published. Based on the stories I heard, it's going to be a great read.

Jon "Jell-O® Boy" Coile Action Figures
Not Available In Stores

Chapter 14

Psycho Safari

In the late spring, Wendy, the consummate shopper, spent $17 Million on a new building for Anne Arundel Community College. The new Center for Applied Learning and Technology building will be nearly 100,000 square feet of classroom and office space when it's finished. The bidding and contract process that consumed Wendy for months at the office, culminated in approval from arch-enemies Governor Parris Glendinning and Comptroller (and former Governor) William Donald Schaeffer at a monthly meeting of the Maryland Board of Public Works.

* * *

Fondly remembering our ride in a seaplane out to Fort Jefferson in the Dry Tortugas, 65 miles from Key West, our plane partner, Mike Baldwin, and I came up with the idea of getting a seaplane as a back-up toy to our Seneca. Recognizing that this plane would be purely for sport, we thought it might be a good idea to get a couple more partners in on the scheme to help share the expense. Mike suggested I talk to my neighbor, Wadi Rahim, owner of a Mooney 201 and an aviation entrepreneur, to find out if he was interested in joining us.

"So, Wadi," I said. "Mike and I are thinking of getting a 25 year-old Lake Amphibian seaplane and we're looking for a couple partners. What do you think?"

"You guys are thinking too small. Let's buy the whole company," Wadi replied.

And with that, Wadi set in motion a series of events that had the three of us, (Mike, Wadi and me), sitting, seven days later, in the corporate offices of Lake Aircraft in Kissimmee, Florida, trying to hammer out a deal with Armand Rivard, the famous aviation impresario who owned the company. Armand has owned Lake Aircraft for 30 years, and at one point he also owned the Mooney Aircraft Corporation too. It's a little known fact that he was the co-father (with the late, great Roy Lopresti) of the first single-engine turbo-prop corporate plane, the Socata TBM 700.

For two days, Armand told us fascinating stories about life in the aviation business during the rollicking times of the 70's. We signed confidentiality agreements so I can't go into many details, but it sounded like it had been a truly great time to be in the business back then.

I was day-dreaming about my legacy in aviation history—Clyde Cessna, Walter Beech, William T. Piper, Jon Coile...

* * *

"Give me a break!" Wendy interrupted my reverie. "Now you are really making stuff up. You weren't going to be anything but a silent partner, and a junior one at that, and you didn't go through with the deal. Wadi's the one who bought the company and got his picture in *Flying* magazine as the new owner of Lake Aircraft. Now get back on track and finish this letter."

* * *

Wendy has an old friend who lives in Massachusetts. Bambi (not her real name) called one day and told Wendy some exciting news. She'd met the man of her dreams in South Africa and they were engaged. Jimmy Johnson (not his real name either, but I love the alliteration and double entendre.) was in the wine business in South Africa and was going to relocate to the United States once they married.

Then Bambi, dropped the big news. She wanted Wendy in her weddings—plural. The first in South Africa and the second one in Massachusetts. Always game for an adventure, we signed up. In addition to the wedding, Bambi offered to book us into a safari camp for four days when we first arrived in Africa, and then a trip to Cape Town for a few days before the wedding. All in all, we would spend two weeks in Africa, leaving for home as the happily married couple departed on their honeymoon.

The flight over was quite the experience. We flew by way of Atlanta, landing for fuel in Cape Town before proceeding on to Jo'burg. Twenty hours in the aircraft, but we were wearing our travelers support socks to avoid economy class syndrome of blood clots in the lower legs.

South Africa was an interesting place. We were surprised to learn that the end of apartheid, the total segregation of all the races, in the early 1990s had not been the end of racial tension. If anything, things might have gotten worse. The residual racial problems aren't as simple as black versus white either, we were to find. There are two main groups of whites, descendants of the English and the Boers, who seem to dislike each other pretty intensely. Then there are at least 11 different tribes of blacks, plus the "Coloreds". We didn't begin to understand the hierarchy of prejudice but got the sense that everybody, in the cities at least, seems to hate and mistrust everybody else, not of their own race, tribe or national origin.

In addition to the underlying structure of mistrust, the economy is in the dumpster. Unemployment approaches 50 % for the majority of blacks. Affirmative action programs are trying to correct the wrongs of centuries but one result of that policy is that career opportunities for university educated young whites are virtually non-existent. It's a bad situation all the way around.

The first time we met Jimmy was when he and Bambi, and her 11 year-old son, picked us up at Johannesburg International Airport. We rented a car and followed them back to the groom's family home. Jimmy and his parents live in a middle class white suburb of Jo'burg, not dissimilar to our own neighborhood in Maryland. We exited the motorway and wound through suburban streets to their townhouse complex. The 20 townhomes were located inside an iron fence, laced with concertina wire—vicious razor wire much more intimidating than ordinary barbed wire. Barbed wire is good enough to keep animals on the right side of fence lines, but if you want to keep out humans, razor wire is the ticket.

We parked the car inside the fence and went up to the next barred gate set securely in a brick wall. Going through this gate got us into an inner courtyard of our townhome. Opening one more gate from the courtyard to the front door gained us access to the solid wood security door. All the security seemed like overkill, but we were new to the country and still naive.

Security seemed to be an overriding concern in the suburbs of Johannesburg. Apparently, immediately prior to the fall of apartheid in the early '90s, some of the Marxist counties in Africa had been helping a guerilla force prepare for civil war, as had happened in Zimbabwe. These military trained, and armed guerillas came back to South Africa ready for a fight that never materialized. Now, facing huge unemployment, some had turned to using their military skills for nefarious purposes. Eight years of home invasions, car jacking, thugs armed with fully automatic assault weapons and C-4 explosive, and bedlam, had left a legacy of near-anarchy. Even the South African airline in-flight magazines, normally full of happy fluff pieces to pass the time in the air, contained articles about how the murder rate of restaurateurs was hurting the hospitality industry. The barred gate on a mall restaurant we ate at, requiring that we be buzzed in like we were entering a high-end jewelry store, was starting to make sense. The street we were staying on, very much like our Benfield Boulevard in Severna Park, was completely deserted of traffic at 6:30 p.m. as everybody got behind locked gates in their respective compounds.

Basically, in light of all this, the general mood over there is that there is not much of a future in South Africa for young whites. They want to get out of the country, like the young whites have already done from Zimbabwe, just to the north. The problem is, over the half century of apartheid, the South Africans had cut themselves off from most of the civilized world. Australia, England, Canada and the U.S. were the places they could go, but each had tight restrictions on immigration, and no real breaks for South Africans. To get to the U.S., there is actually an "immigration lottery" but the sure thing is to marry an American.

Now it was starting to make sense, why a young 30 year-old man would fall instantly in love with a 41 year-old divorcee' with an 11 year-old son, and baggage from her ex. They spent a little over a week together and wham-bam, here's the ring, where's my green card, thank you very much. In fact, Jimmy's sister, we discovered, had already implemented this plan and was living in Charleston, SC with her brand new American husband. The parents told us they were hoping their kids would sponsor their own bid for immigration to the States.

Jimmy apparently felt very threatened by us, and wanted to insulate his green card ticket, Bambi, from any old friend who might point out some of the warning signs. The sordid details are boring, but we ultimately pulled the plug and left a week early, skipping the sham wedding, but, not before we had an incredible four days in the bush on safari.

Here are some of the animal pictures we took on safari at N'Gala, next to the Krueger National Park. Our time in the bush made the entire Africa trip worthwhile.

And just in case you aren't convinced that Jimmy Johnson was the biggest jerk of our experiences in 2002, he firmly believes that the plane crashes on 9/11 were an American plot, orchestrated by President Bush in order to prop up his sagging popularity ratings, and the Al Qaeda are the innocent victims of a CIA smear campaign.

Oh, and by the way, if you want to travel with us in 2003 we need a certificate from your psychiatrist that you've had a recent check-up from the neck-up...

* * *

"That's it. You are done. I'm giving you 200 words to wrap this up."
"But..."
"Now you've only got 199 left. Get cracking."
"Aye, aye, Ma'am."
"You're wasting words. 196 to go."

* * *

Here is the rest of the story:

- Wendy's niece, Noelle, got engaged to her college boyfriend, Blaise. Wedding planned for late summer.
- Ron & Leah, good friends from Israel visited in the fall.
- I'm in two critique groups with local writers, getting excellent feedback as I smooth my waterway book for publication.
- My Brother, Andrew moved home to go back to college for a Bachelors and Masters in Computer Science. The Folks are enjoying having him back under their roof.
- Whitney Paige Miles Cameron Dirtball Scumbag, the scam artist who swindled my parents, is working his way through the court process. Amazingly he was acquitted on criminal charges, but I guess I shouldn't be surprised. It's the same California court system that acquitted O.J. Civil trials to follow.
- In June, a month after I met him, Bret Hart fell while riding his bicycle. He hit his head on the ground, suffered another concussion and had a massive stroke. As I write this, the news on the internet has him recovering in Calgary and the prognosis is good.
- Both our families are fine and doing well.

And so, with only 11 words left, we wish you Merry Christmas and Happy New...

Christmas—2003

Teaching the Diary of
snow
falls
on
coiles

Christmas—2003
snow
falls
on
coiles

a Christmas letter
in haiku
from jon &
wendy

snow falls on coiles
cold way to start the new year
jon and wendy weep

well, not really weep
maybe snivel a little
pine for warm weather

this haiku stuff is
kind of hard for me to get
syllables just right

Chapter 15

Haiku

"What in the Wide World of Sports do you think you are doing?" Wendy barked. "This is your attempt at our Christmas Letter? Are you insane?"

"But, Snookums," an even-tempered Jon replied. "Since you didn't like last year's letter I thought I would write this one in Haiku. You know—three lines of Japanese poetry with five, then seven, then five syllables. I was doing it for you, Snookie Wookie."

"Why wouldn't I like last year's letter? I think I was in almost two complete paragraphs of the 32 pages, Mr. Jell-O-boy®."

"Hey," Jon replied reasonably. "Last Christmas I was just beginning to develop my writer's voice. This time I'll make sure you get at least seventeen pages. I'll even throw in you making some gestures to amplify your dialogue and give real depth to your character."

"Generous offer, but no deal," Wendy said, emphatically shaking her tightly balled fist vigorously under Jon's nose. "I'm writing this year's letter."

"But, but, Precious...I've been working on my iambic pentameter. I was going to tell the moose story in the style of..."

"Get." The sinister one word command struck fear deep in the bowels of the fledgling writer. "And take your excessive use of adverbs ending in-ly with you!"

* * *

This year was an eventful one in the Coile household. Some good, some bad, and some...well, let us just tell you what happened and you decide for yourself.

Oh, and by the way, even though my husband obviously doesn't get it, there is much more to writing Haiku than just putting enough syllables in each line. As any basic fifth grade student of poetry knows, good Haiku evokes a mood of the season without explicitly stating the emotion to be felt. "Jon and Wendy weep because it's cold." How lame. Try a winter in Rochester. But I digress. Back to our Christmas Letter.

"See, Honey," Jon calmly countered. "These little digressions are addictive. If you aren't careful this letter will be even longer than last year."

"Get out of here, and go chop some wood or something. I've got this letter under control."

Jon sulked his way down the stairs and headed for the wood shed to collect his ax while Wendy continued at her efforts on the computer.

* * *

February: The Gypsy Acupuncturist

In Jacksonville two years ago, while playing in a casual volleyball game at one of Jon's business meetings I jumped up to hit the ball when...POW...something impacted me hard, right in the back of my leg. I landed in a heap.

* * *

"Let me tell this part," Jon said, putting his ax down next to the computer. "I know it was your injury, but can I please write about it?"

"Can I trust you to keep it short, on topic and truthful?"

"Definitely", Jon replied, sitting down at the computer, with a covert little wink to Leo, perched on top of the mini-tower.

Chapter 16

Unlicensed Gypsy Acupuncturist

When she limped off the court, I comforted Wendy. "What happened?"

"That old son-of-a-bitch over there kicked me in my leg!" Wendy replied, grimacing in agony as she gestured at the soon-to-be-retired President of a sleepy little southern mortgage company.

I glanced at the Captain Kangaroo-esque character, still out on the court playing an exceedingly passive form of old-man-volleyball, unaware of Wendy's anger or pain. Her claim didn't seem plausible.

"He kicked you?"

"He either kicked me, or kicked one of those nuts into my leg," Wendy replied, angry at being doubted. She pointed to the plethora of black walnuts littering the ground. "It feels like I got hit by a golf ball."

Three hours later we were told by the Jacksonville Memorial Emergency Room Physician that Wendy tore her calf muscle when she pushed off from the uneven ground to jump for the ball, an injury that can feel just like being hit in the leg by a golf ball. Apparently Capt. Kangaroo was innocent.

Several doctors, lots of physical therapy, deep tissue massage, the passage of nearly two years of continuous rehabilitation, and still the injury stubbornly refused to mend. At wit's end, Wendy was ready to try anything.

Finding a Chinese-American surgeon who dabbled in Eastern Medicine on the side, Wendy signed up for a session of "Wet Acupuncture." More commonly known in the western hemisphere as "Prolotherapy", wet acupuncture involves injecting a glucose solution right into the heart of soft tissue injuries. The body, sensing the invading foreign substance responds by sending blood, antibodies, and other mystical energy right to the site of the injection. Finding nothing there but benign glucose, the blood and stuff go to work fixing whatever else needs attention, allegedly making the soft tissues stronger. Wendy didn't know if it would work, but decided to give it a try.

* * *

I was wrapping up some things in my office the evening of the prolotherapy session when my cell phone rang.

"When are you going to get here?" Wendy said without preamble, clearly in some discomfort.

"Thirty minutes. I'll pick you up at seven as we planned."

"Well the doctor wants you here now."

"I'm on my way."

No higher priority than the health of loved ones, I thought, as I headed for the parking lot. As my car surged down the dark boulevard, swallowing up the black asphalt, the cell phone rang again.

"Where are you?"

"Passing *Fishpaws*. There in ten minutes." The tumbledown liquor store slid past my drivers-side window as I took the curve towards Annapolis.

"Okay. Just hurry."

I picked up the pace, concentrating on my driving and soon reached the office. As I walked into the dimly lit waiting room, I was surprised to find it completely empty. No nurse, no receptionist, no signs of my wife.

"Back here," a gentle voice called from the bowels of the office. "Take off your coat and come on back."

I did as commanded and when I got to the examining room I found my wife laying face down on a table, waiting patiently for me with the Doctor.

"We're got something you need to learn. It will help Wendy with her recovery," the Doctor said after brief introductions.

"Oh?"

"I'm going to do the heavy lifting, so to speak—wet acupuncture treatments, about three weeks apart. In between those treatments you need to do dry acupuncture every night."

Wet? Dry? Acupuncture? Me? My blank stare must have been proof that this was happening faster than I could comprehend.

Brushing aside my anxiety, over the next fifteen minutes the good Doctor gave me all the training he felt I needed to be competent in basic acupuncture techniques for leg injuries, and then sent us on our way.

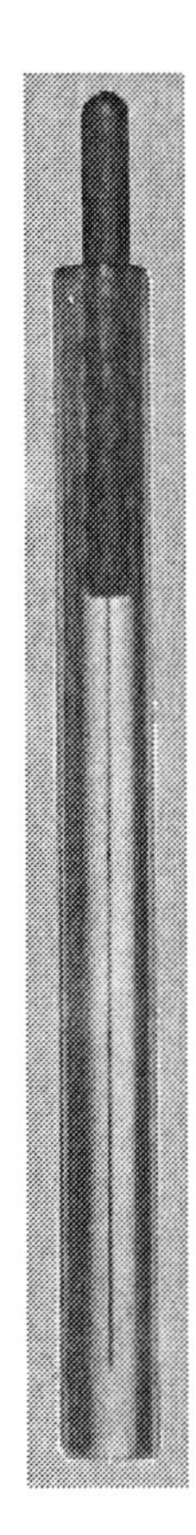

The next night, after dinner, Wendy was ready for me to administer her first treatment. Looking over her leg I tried hard to remember all I had learned. Let's see: Wipe down my hands with alcohol pads. Wipe her leg with more pads. Twist the needle in the insertion sleeve to break it free. Rest the tip of the insertion sleeve on her leg with the needle pointed down and with a smart tap of the index finger on the end of the handle—sink that needle deep into her flesh. I took a deep breath and gave the first needle its smart tap.

"WHAT ARE YOU DOING?!!!" Wendy provided me with instant feedback I wasn't on the right track.

"Uh, just trying to do what the doctor showed me."

"Well that sure as hell didn't feel like what he did last night."

"Sorry."

"You need to tell me what you are doing every step of the way before you start jamming needles in my leg."

Wendy and I worked out a system. As she tells it, I start off by alerting her with, "Here comes a little prick."

That is absolutely not true. I say, "Here comes a little stick." S-t-i-c-k.

After the initial stick, I give her feedback as to how far the needle has sunk into her leg. The needles are as thin as a human hair and about an inch and a half long, plus a little plastic handle. I usually only insert the needle about an inch into her leg, giving continuous status reports the whole way in: Thirty percent...fifty percent...eighty percent...done. I run a pattern of five needles down her leg, from mid-calf to the Achilles tendon, twisting them every three minutes for a total treatment time of fifteen minutes. Then out they come, and into a "sharps" bio-hazard disposal container.

The second night we did the acupuncture, the insertion operation went a bit smoother. After the fifteen minutes of twisting it came time to pull the needles. The first one slid right out like it was greased. For some reason, the second one tugged back, the calf muscle gripping the acupuncture needle tightly from deep inside her leg. I didn't know what to do.

I broke the bad news to Wendy. "The needle won't come out."

"Just pull it."

"Are you sure?"

"PULL IT!"

Against my better judgment, I gave a colossal tug, and after a brief fight the needle popped out of her leg. I took one look and just about passed out. The ditty from *The Beverly Hillbillies* started playing in my head:

"And up from the ground comes a bubblin' crude.
Oil that is.
Black gold.
Texas tea."

Only this stuff was red!

My finger flashed forward and slammed down on the mushrooming droplet.

"Am I bleeding?" She asked.

"Oh, just a little," I lied. "It's nothing."

Quickly yanking the other needles, my finger kept pressure on the well-head. After about a minute, I snuck a peak at the gusher. Much to my surprise, it had stopped—a black cloud under the skin indicating a bruise was forming.

We slogged on for three more weeks with nightly sessions, Wendy feeling that my semi-competent efforts as an unlicensed gypsy acupuncturist were actually helping the healing process.

As the date approached for her next prolotherapy session, I could hardly wait. As soon as we were in the door, I peppered the doctor with questions.

"There is so much I should have asked you when I was here last time," I started. "What exactly is inside this leg? Am I going to hit a nerve by accident and launch Wendy right through the ceiling of our bedroom? What if I hit an artery? Or a bone? Can I do any damage with these needles? I really don't know what the hell I'm doing."

"Oh, yeah. I should have told you a few other things," the doctor concurred, as he launched into a fifteen minute anatomy lesson.

I could tell you what he said, but that would make this into a combination Christmas Letter/Medical Textbook and really, *something* has to be beyond the scope of this letter.

The end of the story is that acupuncture and prolotherapy worked. Wendy's leg has healed and she is back exercising. We've both lost weight on the Doctor's secret acupuncture weight loss scheme and our health is pretty good at this point. I've even trained Wendy to do acupuncture on herself, so I rarely have to exercise my skills anymore.

And that, Ladies and Gentlemen, is fine by me.

* * *

It's not bad," said Wendy, setting the draft manuscript down on the kitchen table.

"I don't know," replied Jon. "I'm a little depressed about this letter."

"Why."

"It just seems flat after last year's effort. Not as snappy. It even seems almost boring."

"Well maybe that's because nobody has tried to kill us yet. No Captain Morgan types, or idiots leading us astray in darkest Africa."

"Well, that's true."

"Pace yourself. You are only up to February. I'm sure there is more exciting stuff to write about in the months ahead. Just keep going, but maybe you could try and make it quicker. These people have holiday parties to go to and can't take all day reading our letter. Try and aim more for Hemingway and less like Michener."

"I'm on it!" I replied, excited to be allowed to write our letter without further attempts to take away my keyboard.

Chapter 17

A Blur of Activity

March—Our Best Friend

Ten years ago, Wendy was working out of our house running her family elevator business. Being a bit lonely she decided we should get a dog. As many of you know, we adopted a 6-year-old Golden Retriever from the Golden Retriever Rescue organization.

When we got Keesha, she weighed 95 pounds and her fur was falling out in clumps. Once on the correct thyroid medication, and under Wendy's loving care, Keesha slimmed down to a trim 67 pounds, and grew a luxurious coat of golden hair.

Keesha always thought of herself as a people person. Willing to play with other dogs, she preferred the company of humans, and none more than Wendy.

Most people are familiar with the concept of dogs aging seven years for every calendar year, but that doesn't quite apply for the larger breeds. After ten years, they age more rapidly, and rarely go much beyond twelve or fourteen. When Keesha celebrated her sixteenth birthday in February, we knew we didn't have much time left.

She went over the Rainbow Bridge quietly, with both of us by her side, on April 1st, leaving a big hole in our family.

* * *

April—Captain Action

We have a friend, Jeff Eckel, who has become terrified of appearing in our Christmas Letter. He is especially fearful of getting branded with a nickname like "Richard Head" or "Capt. Morgan". It actually keeps him on his best behavior throughout the year. Well this year, Jeff...

(Insert funny story here about Jeff Eckel, AKA Captain Action.)

"Where are you going with this?" Wendy asked.

"I don't know." I admitted.

"Well knock it off. Quit pandering to your readers and get back to the story."

"Yes, Ma'am," I replied.

* * *

April—The Phone Call

I was working in my office one afternoon when the receptionist called back. She had a phone call for my brother, Chris. An old friend of his needed to speak to him urgently. Chris being out of town, our receptionist wanted to know if I would take the call.

"Send it through," I replied.

"Jon, this is Art Ebersberger. I'm over in Cambridge with the Board of Directors of Anne Arundel Medical Center at a meeting with your brother, Russ. He's having some sort of medical problem and they are taking him to Easton Memorial Hospital. I'm trying to reach anybody in the family."

Art filled me in on the sketchy details, as he knew them. Apparently, after lunch, while speaking to the hospital board in his role as a Health Futurist, Russ had an episode of expressive aphasia. He could hear things said to him with complete clarity but his reply was jumbled, his words not making sense. They didn't know what was causing it and were taking him to the hospital to check it out.

I wrote down Art's cell phone number and ran for my car with just my palm pilot and cell phone. My first call was to Russ' mother, Peg, in Annapolis.

"We need to go to Easton Hospital. Russ is meeting us there in an ambulance. Don't know what the problem is yet but he's got the chief neurosurgeon from Anne Arundel with him. I'll pick you up in fifteen minutes." I said.

Next call was to Wendy. "We need to track down Nancy in Texas and Zac in D.C." Russ' wife and son needed to be brought in on this.

Russ was fortunate to have his problem while speaking before the leadership team of a great hospital, and with friends in the audience. The CEO of Anne Arundel got on the phone to his counterpart at Easton Memorial to get things in motion. When his ambulance arrived at the E.R., Russ was whisked in for an immediate cat scan. Within 20 minutes of arriving, they had determined he was not having a stroke, and had reloaded him into the ambulance for further transport to Anne Arundel for more tests and evaluation.

The ambulance was idling at the Emergency Room entrance waiting for us as we pulled up. Peg jumped out of my car and into the ambulance, and with the neurosurgeon's BMW in convoy, our three vehicles headed back to Annapolis.

Zac, Russ' son and a reporter in the D.C. Bureau of the San Francisco Chronicle met us at the hospital. After a few hours of tests we were able to get in to see Russ. They weren't sure exactly what was happening but thought they saw a dark spot on his brain at the part that controls speech. They wanted him to stay over for more tests.

The next day he checked out of the hospital and flew home to Texas to consult with his own doctor, and be with Nancy.

* * *

May—Coby & Kelly

After the loss of Keesha, and a waiting period of a couple months, Wendy decided we needed to get not one, but two dogs. Back we went to GRREAT, the Golden Retriever rescue organization. Even though we were prior rescue dog owners we had to re-apply and go through a rigorous screening process. The six page application satisfied most of the screening committee's questions but we still had to go through a home inspection by a committee member, accompanied by a "screening dog." They wanted to see how we behaved with an actual dog in our home before they would entrust another one of their rescued animals to us.

I was upstairs taking a shower the Saturday morning when the screener arrived. I came down to find Wendy talking animatedly with the screener, and her nine-year-old golden, Maggie. Wendy was clearly anxious about presenting just the right image. They were discussing Maggie's health, and the difficulty in keeping her weight down, a problem Keesha had shared for the last couple years of her life.

"Is it okay if I give Maggie one of these?" I enquired innocently, holding up a butter flavored rice cake, the low-cal replacement for dog biscuits we had given Keesha.

"I think that would be all right," the screener replied.

"Chomp," Maggie said as she inhaled the rice cake, and then plopped down in contentment for a rest right on top of my feet.

With a flourish the screener put a big check mark on our application form.

* * *

We started the rounds of adoption days, meeting available dogs currently living in foster homes, and checking the GRREAT website daily for more potential dog listings. At our third adoption day we met Coby, a five-year-old blond male.

He was sitting on the floor of the pet store, surrounded by 20 other dogs up for adoption, with a crowd of 50 to 60 people all eagerly petting every available furry head. He looked like he was tired of people as he wiggled in behind his foster mom.

"He seems a bit passive," Wendy commented as we watched him lying still on the floor as other dogs around him jumped and barked and pulled on their leashes.

Perfect, I thought, as he moved his head back into the open and made eye contact with me. Through very intelligent eyes he clearly conveyed, *Get me out of this bedlam. Please.*

"We want this one," I said. Coby smiled up at me with a big toothy grin. "Definitely."

Two weeks of negotiation with the foster family later and he was ours, on one condition: we had to get a second dog so Coby would have a companion. As that played right along with Wendy's plan, we agreed.

Six weeks later Wendy came up with Kelly, a three-year-old nearly red golden female. Higher energy than Coby, Kelly is more like a dog in personality than the little person in a dog suit that we were used to with Keesha and Coby. While Coby is a Velcro® dog, staying close to our side no matter where we are in the house, Kelly can usually be found at a window, scanning for squirrels, ducks or geese to chase if she could just figure out these pesky door knobs.

Coby, Kelly, Schooner and Keel attending a prayer breakfast. (Praying for dog biscuits.)

* * *

May—Surgery

In May, Russ was back up in Annapolis. He had received a second opinion from the doctors at the University of Texas Hospital in Austin, and they concurred with the ones in Maryland. They all thought there was a brain tumor growing on his speech center and it needed to be taken out. Russ picked Annapolis and came up for the procedure.

Three days after the surgery we met up with Russ and Nancy for dinner at Northwoods in West Annapolis. If we hadn't known, we wouldn't have guessed that he had been under the knife not 72 hours earlier. Using a technique that must have been inspired by the Indians in old Westerns, they had just sort of temporarily moved everything out of their way when they went in to cut out the brain tumor. Replacing everything when done, presto, Russ looked like his usual self.

Over dinner we talked about a manuscript for a golf novel a writer friend of mine had given me for feedback. As Russ is the author of the family, with ten published books and a golf novel of his own in final editing, I'd passed it on to him to look over while recuperating. As we dined on crab cakes and a good California chardonnay, Russ gave me some suggestions to take back to my writer friend. His perceptions of where the book needed to be improved was a clear indicator his brain was banging on all cylinders again.

Wendy and I were heartened at his progress as we parted; Russ and Nancy leaving in the morning to drive to Boston to see Russ' newborn first grandchild—Nathaniel.

* * *

The Summer—A Blur of Activity.

In June, while I was visiting my parents in California, we received sad news. Norah, my mother's sister in Australia, had passed away. Always a vibrant, funny lady, and one of our favorite aunts, she will be missed.

In the three years since I scared the snot out of myself in a thunderstorm over Kalamazoo, Michigan, I've been thinking of taking an instrument flying simulator course to hone my skills. This year I finally did it. I got to spend three days jammed into a little black phone booth sized cubicle, technically known as a Piper Seneca Twin Engine Flight Simulator. It was continuous action: engines catching fire, landing gear jammed, gyros failing, radios breaking, and all while flying night instrument approaches in truly evil weather—it was total chaos. The sick bastard

I had for a flight instructor wrung me out, and left me drenched with sweat, but made me a better pilot in the process.

The rest of our summer was filled with weddings and family reunions. In early August, Wendy's niece Noelle married her college sweetheart Blaise, in a beautiful wedding in Syracuse, New York. The church was hot, the wine was cold, family and friends were plentiful, and it was a beautiful and well orchestrated wedding week-end celebration.

After the wedding, many in Wendy's family headed up to Clayton, NY in the Thousand Islands of the St. Lawrence Seaway for a few days of sailing, swimming and fun.

Returning to Maryland, the sun, the moon and the stars all came together at once and seventeen Coiles, Craigs and Veales all converged at Chris & Susie's for a family picnic. The Champion croquet match was the highlight for many.

We ended the summer by celebrating the wedding of our friends, Fred & Deb Nizer. Their nuptials turned into an entire week-end of events, centered on the Bleu Rock Inn in the hunt country of Virginia, right up in the foothills of the Shenandoah.

Sitting next to the Bleu Rock's polo field was a huge blue bird. I hardly paid it any attention as we rushed hither and yon for the various wedding events. If I had realized that this bird might foreshadow our entrée to the world of Wal-mart and Cracker Barrel, I would definitely have slowed down and looked it over. But I missed the chance, never dreaming of the looming crisis that would send us charging down a new path in life.

* * *

September—Hurricane Isabel

September 19th, just after midnight, our alarm clock started ringing. Wendy and I got up in the darkness and flipped the light switch.

"Nothing." I stated the obvious. The power was dead. The hurricane winds pounding on the windows were yanking trees out of the rain saturated ground, bringing down power lines all over Maryland.

A flash light beam swept our bedroom. "Here's a light," Wendy said, passing me the torch. We moved to the stairs, curious to see what was happening outside.

"High tide in twenty minutes," I said as we walked through the back yard to our pier. Spray lashed us as we huddled in the lee of our neighbor's three-story home. I trained my light on the water and all we could see were gray-black waves marching past in the darkness. Our pier was underwater, even the tops of the pilings, 24 inches above the pier decking, were invisible beneath the stormy waters.

"Has it peaked?" Wendy asked.

"I hope so." I replied as we watched the water lapping within an inch of the top of our concrete seawall. Within a few minutes we could tell that the water had crested with the tide and was heading back down. We returned to bed, convinced we had survived Hurricane Isabel in the dark, but without a scratch.

* * *

"Oh, my god!" Wendy woke me from a deep slumber a little after 6:30 am. "Look outside."

I rolled out of bed and looked out the window at the early dawn twilight. Our back yard was flooded, the river having defied the tide tables and risen more than two feet from the level at midnight.

"The wind shifted," I said with a glance at the wavelets on the river.

"It's coming out of the south now, pushing the water up the bay. The eye of the hurricane must have passed us."

We jumped into our clothes and

ran outside. The water was still safely away from our home, but was flooding our neighbors property, creating navigable water where previously only riding lawnmowers dared to tread.

"I'm launching my kayak!" Wendy said, running for her paddle and life jacket in the basement.

"Get mine too." I called, pulling our two boats off the high ground next to the house, and down to the new beach in the middle of our yard.

For an hour, we kayaked around the front yards of our neighborhood. Steering between trees, making channels around lawn sheds, we stayed in close, out of the gusts of wind on the main body of the river. Neighbors poured out of their houses, and with the exception of some minor outbuildings, there was no significant damage in our immediate neighborhood. It was a festive atmosphere, much like the morning after a two foot snowfall.

After an hour of play the water started to recede. The wind dropped as well, which was fortunate as we had a plane to catch. Onward to our crisis.

Chapter 18

The Mid-life Crisis

The Crisis

Right before the Hurricane roared up the bay, I suddenly had a mid-life crisis. Well, not really a crisis, but sort of an itch. The kind that can only be satisfied by buying something big and mechanical on Ebay. I looked around and hit on it.

"Snookums, do you know what a Unimog is?" I enquired innocently?

"A Uni-what?"

"Mog," I replied. "A Unimog is an industrial strength 4x4 made by Mercedes. It's like the Arnold Schwarzenegger of off road vehicles. Makes a Hummer look like a pansy."

"No I don't know what one is, but since we aren't getting one, it doesn't really matter."

Drat.

I headed back to the computer to surf Ebay for something else.

I've had this little affliction ever since somebody told me about the cylinder game. For guys, my new friend told me, life is all about cylinders. How many internal combustion engine cylinders do you have in all your toys combined. I did my math:

Toy	Total Cylinders
My Car	8
Wendy's Car	6
Airplane	12 (Two 6-cylinder engines)
Boat	16 (Two V-8s. WhooHoooo!)
Lawnmower	1 (Sort of broken, but it still counts)
New Toy TBD	*TBD*
Total	**43 now, aiming for 50+!**

Then I found it! I wanted—no, *needed*—an RV! With an eight cylinder diesel main engine, and a four banger generator this would put my total score to a manly 55!

After countless hours of research over about two days I figured out that the only RV for me would be a Blue Bird Wanderlodge. Built like a brick outhouse by the Blue Bird School Bus Company of Fort Valley, Georgia, these galvanized steel behemoths are designed to be able to roll over an embankment with a bus load of kids and bounce back without a scratch. (Ever wonder why school buses don't have any seat belts at all, but you will go to jail if you don't have your kids strapped down in a NASA engineered four-point-harness lunar module child seat to carry them to McDonalds in your average SUV?)

Blue Bird started making high-end motorhomes out of their galvanized school bus chassis in the early '60s. Built like the land yacht version of a Bertram or Hatteras, they are the epitome of luxury. When I found out that Tom Cruise has one of these babies, I was hooked. Searching in earnest, I was trying to find one that would be perfect for me, Wendy, two cats and two dogs. I rationalized that we could use it to go to Key West for Christmas. Amazingly, Wendy bought off on this scheme. What a wife!

We ultimately found a twenty year old Blue Bird Wanderlodge Forward Control 35 Side Bath in Holland, Michigan. It is thirty-five feel long and looks like a Rock Star coach from the Earth Tone/Disco Era!

These Wanderlodges are frequently given names by their owners. My first suggestion was:

"Midvale School for the Gifted"

Nobody seemed to get the Gary Larsen cartoon reference, so I decided this was just a little too subtle for our huge school bus look-alike. My second suggestion was:

"**No Way** are we buying a twenty-year-old RV on Ebay, sight unseen!"

Which of course was exactly what we had just done.

At this point, Wendy took over naming privileges and came up with the perfect choice, using the following logic: It's big. It's brown. It makes us smile. So we have nicknamed our Blue Bird Wanderlodge:

"The Moose."

Driving a bus that weighs as much as ten standard cars; accelerates like a clapped out Yugo; stops like your brakes just gave out, and maneuvers like a sumo wrestler in a Lladro shop, does take some getting used to. We definitely feel a kindred spirit with the long distance truck drivers and their big rigs.

Just in case we feel we aren't getting enough attention with our flashy metallic brown paint job, Blue Bird has sensibly installed a device they call, "The Horn". It is a huge speaker system that plays more than 60 songs. I haven't heard them all YET since Wendy cut me off after about 20 or 30. So far we have discovered everything from the William Tell Overture to the theme from Rocky. We are like an ice cream truck on steroids when we cruise through the neighborhood playing the hot hits of 1983 at 100+ decibels!

We will keep you posted on our experiences in the RV world, but so far it's a lot of fun. And yes we eat at Cracker Barrel, (they have special parking for RVs and let us sleep over in their lot), and shop at Wal-mart (Have you seen their prices?! Unbelievable! They also allow RV slumber parties in the parking lot. The polite thing to do is to go in and buy a bottle of Yoo-hoo and a couple Moon Pies first like any good customer before you bed down for the night.)

This RV stuff is really a gas.

* * *

October—Russ visits Annapolis

My brother Russ is a big car nut. Hot rods, sports cars, anything with wheels. When he came through town on a business trip to see his mom and check in with the doctors, we made arrangements to meet for dinner at The Melting Pot, a fondue restaurant. Fondue is a great way to spend a relaxing evening. Wendy and I decided to surprise Russ by driving to dinner in "The Moose."

"What engine do you have?" Russ asked, after an appreciative tour.

"Caterpillar 3208 Turbo Diesel," I proudly replied.

"If you want to get more power out of that engine, it doesn't really cost that much to increase the size of the injectors and install a bigger turbo," he suggested.

We talked over different modifications I might pursue, and the benefits and pitfalls of each, as we dipped bread into the cheese fondue pot in the middle of our table.

"There's a very nice merlot on the wine list you should try, Wendy," Russ, the knowledgeable connoisseur suggested, flagging down our waiter. "Could we please get a bottle of the Dynamite from Carmenet."

We talked about cars, and wine, and life and family, never touching on his looming health issues. They were out there, of course, but talking about them wouldn't make them any better. Russ was attacking his cancer with optimism, and being optimistic too, we supported him in that.

After dinner, the three of us went and sat in The Moose. With an air suspension system, and air brakes, we need to start the big diesel and let it idle for a few minutes to charge up the air flasks before getting underway. We sat in the salon as the big Cat clattered beneath our feet, savoring the manly smells and sounds of heavy machinery. When the air system pressurized to 75 psi, we were ready to go. After a hug goodbye, Russ opened the side door and climbed down the air-operated steps to the ground.

As Wendy and I pulled out of the parking lot, I dialed up song #2A on "The Horn". Russ looked back from the door of his rental car and smiled at us as the sounds of "On the Road Again" blasted across the parking lot.

With a woosh of air brakes, and a roar from the diesel, Wendy and I took off with a final wave as we hit the highway.

* * *

October: The Surprise

In October, Chris and I traveled to Des Moines, Iowa for our quarterly Board Meeting and CEO retreat with the leadership teams of our sister companies in the HomeServices real estate empire.

At the start of the meeting, Chris totally surprised me by announcing that he was promoting me to President of Champion Realty, Inc. He also announced that he was taking the role of Chairman/Chief Executive Officer of the Champion/Chancellor family of companies. It isn't as much a change in responsibilities, but more an acknowledgement of the roles we are both currently taking in our company. A good thing for both of us.

We have been working together for fifteen years, and Chris has taught me an unbelievable amount in business. I'm very grateful for the role he has let me play with Champion. Second smartest thing I ever did was coming to work with Chris. (Marrying Wendy was the smartest.)

* * *

November—Russ

A couple weeks after we had dinner with Russ in The Moose, he went into the hospital in Texas to take care of a staph infection that had taken hold in his leg. With an immune system weakened by cancer and chemo, the doctors worked hard to battle the infection so he would be out for his surprise 60th birthday party on Saturday. It wasn't to be. His whole family had flown in for the gathering, so the party moved to the hospital. It was a festive time, under the circumstances.

He passed away two weeks later, in mid-November. It's a very sad time for all of us and we miss him.

Chapter 19

A Sad December

December—...

We are going to Key West for Christmas, sharing the coach with Coby and Kelly, and our two cats, Leo and Pauline.

We've got a little wine cellar in The Moose. When we get to Key West we are going to sit on the sand in front of our coach and pull a bottle of Dynamite Merlot out of that little wine cellar and have a drink to Russ, and Norah, and Keesha, and all the rest of our family and friends. We'll count our blessing for the people we have in our lives. Know that we'll be thinking of you, when we are down there.

Christmas—2004

Chapter 20

The BluePrint®

INFORMATION STATEMENT:

1. Greetings Sender: Jon & Wendy Coile

GENERAL NOTES:

1. Any deviation from/or in-field alteration to these Holiday Greetings/specifications is strictly prohibited without prior approval of Santa Claus.
2. Do not scale drawings for any purpose. Contact Elf Engineering if additional dimensions are required.

INTRODUCTION:

"I was looking at a listing of yours," the young kid sitting next to me said, as we sat in the Board Room of the Maryland Association of Realtors, waiting for a meeting to start.

"Oh, which one, Tommy?" I replied, casually wondering if he was going to be old enough soon to drop the 'mee' and go with just plain old Tom. That wasn't a very charitable thought I knew, as both Tommy, and his dad 'Big Tommy' before him had been using the name as a personal brand in the real estate industry in Maryland for many years. Little Tommy was my counterpart as President of another real estate company. He may have been in the first half of his 30s, and I in the last half of my 40s, but in my mind we were pretty close to being contemporaries.

"A waterfront in Annapolis," Tommy continued, telling me which one. I knew the property instantly as it was so magnificent it didn't just have an address; it had a name. Kind of like Monticello, The White House, or Donald Trump's Mar-a-Lago.

"Who's looking?" I asked. "You or your dad?"

"Me. I just got married and want a house to raise a family. It's a beautiful property but won't work for us. I really want to build if I can find the right waterfront lot."

As I drove away after the meeting, I thought about young Tommy's situation. Like many people, he was following the typical buying patterns for real estate. First home in the 25–29 year-old range. First move-up five to seven years later in your mid-30s. Last move up between ages 43 and 46. First move down in the mid-50s. Again at retirement. Then the Independent Living-Assisted Living-Nursing Home track to...HOLY HELL! My 47th birthday was three months away! The last move-up window was slamming shut on me! If I don't go now, I never will!

My eyes snapped to the left. No traffic in the rear view mirror. I cranked my car into a u-turn and roared off south out of Annapolis. McMansions were popping up like mushrooms after a soaking rain in the horse country of Davidsonville. I needed to get into one *now*, and see what we were missing.

* * *

"Hey! Remember me?" Wendy asked as she peered over my shoulder at our Christmas Letter slowly taking shape on the computer monitor.

"Sorry, Snookums, I was just trying to explain the origin of this year's Xmas Letter theme."

"Are you writing another self-centered, narcissistic, epic of aggrandizement, pretending it's our holiday letter?" she asked.

"Hey, watch your language, little Miss Thesaurus. I'm trying to keep my Flesch-Kincaid reading level score down in elementary school."

"What are you talking about?"

"Well my writer's group keeps pinging on me that nobody has time to read my excessively verbose Christmas Letter so I decided if I use really basic English, then people could read it fast without thinking too hard."

"I've got a brand new concept for you, writer-boy. Keep it short. This year you get one page. That's it. Write pithily."

"Pithily? What the hell is that?" I asked as I launched my Internet browser. Google quickly returned:

Pithily—ADJECTIVE: Consisting of or resembling pith.

"Keep reading, you illiterate." Wendy pointed to the bottom of the screen. "Scroll down. Pithily in this context means, 'Precisely meaningful; forceful and brief.' Emphasis on *brief*. You get one page."

As she left the room, I thought about my options. I could either try and write pithily, or I could use 11 x 17 paper. It would be really difficult for me to edit down to that small a document, but if I used 7-point type and crunched the margins...then it hit me. My solution was in chemicals. Ammonia to be exact.

For Christmas 2004 I would write one big, mongo, huge page of ammonia-reeking, action-crammed prose, printed first to velum, and then chemically etched on to a single sheet of **BluePrint®**. One thousand two hundred and sixty square inches of Holiday Cheer. That just might be enough.

* * *

"Let me give you the ground rules for this year's Christmas Letter," Wendy said sternly.

"Ground rules?" Jon inquired innocently.

"Ground rules," she continued. "Let's start with adverb usage. We're just going to 'say' stuff. No 'said sternly', or 'inquired innocently'. We are just going to talk like normal people."

"Bu, bu, but..."

"Give me a break!" Wendy said. "What kind of lame dialogue are you experimenting with now? Don't try and tell me. I don't care. Back to the ground rules. You get three stories and that's it. No day-by-day, hour-by-hour, minute-by-minute journal of every little tiny thing that happened to us in 2004. Just three stories—on one page."

"Oh, come on."

"If you don't pick the stories, I will. You get to write about moose, house and family."

"What about God and Country?"

"What about Hallmark cards with pre-printed holiday greetings?"

"Moose, house and family, aye aye, Ma'am. I'm on it."

Chapter 21

The Moose

If you are a serial reader of our Xmas letters, you know that last year we bought an old motorhome on Ebay, (a Bluebird Wanderlodge), with the express intention of using it for a trip to Key West for Christmas. Our plan was to take us, our two golden retrievers, our two cats, and with Wendy's car in tow run down the East Coast to the next-to-the-last Key on U.S. Route One. We had a spot reserved for a week at the 'famous' Boyd's Campground on Beautiful Stock Island. Or should I say, the 'infamous' Boyd's Campground...but I get ahead of myself.

The first change in plan was with the dogs. After Keesha passed away in the spring of 2003, we got Coby from the Golden Retriever rescue. A five-year-old male with the sensitive spirit of an artist, he had settled in to our family just fine, getting along great with the cats after he figured out what a cat was. He adapted well to his position in the pecking order of our pack.

Fundamentally, dogs are pack animals, running in packs with a defined hierarchy. The leader of the pack is the "Alpha" dog. In our little animal herd, "Alpha" is unquestionably, always, and unequivocally...Wendy.

Our last Golden, Keesha, adopted the role of "Bravo". Wendy's First Lieutenant. The XO. Her Chief of Staff. Leo, our Maine Coon cat was "Charlie", right behind Keesha. That meant that bringing up the rear, Pauline, our black cat from Key West, and I sort of shared the "Delta" slot. Actually, at the advanced age of 16, Pauline doesn't really play in this pack game, preferring to just sleep under the covers for 20 hours a day like Martha Stuart and other inmates. This left me pretty much undisputed for the title "Delta Dog".

The problem with being Delta Dog is that when I tell the Bravo Dog to do something, it is really just a suggestion from a peer. Like one of your buddies asking you if you want to go out for a beer. If you feel like it, "Yeah, I'll do that."

Now on the other hand, when Alpha speaks, "All hail the Empress of the Universe." Eat, poop, fetch, sit, stay, roll over. "Ma'am, Aye-Aye, Ma'am, Yes, Ma'am. Right now. Ma'am."

When Coby joined us, there was a brief tussle for power and Leo claimed "Bravo", Coby became "Charlie" and Pauline and I stayed down in our familiar "Delta Dog" position. Then we introduced Kelly, a three-year-old Golden to the pack.

Kelly was very bright, but stubborn as a little 63-pound Ox. She didn't want to merely be higher than Coby and above all cats. Kelly felt her rightful role was ahead of *everybody* as the new "Alpha Coile".

You can imagine how far that got with Wendy. Coby was equally not in favor of regime change, and spent a lot of energy trying to explain to Kelly that she must accept her new role as Delta, tossing Pauline and me under the bus and down to the role of Echo and Foxtrot.

* * *

"Bus! Bus! Bus!" Wendy interrupted me at the computer. "Finally! Five hundred and fifty three words into the Moose story and you finally mention the word bus, but you aren't even talking about OUR bus. What exactly are you doing, Mr. Ramblin' Man?" Wendy asked.

"I was just getting to the Moose part."

When we departed for the Christmas trip we left Kelly at home with friends Fred & Beth. (F&B: Thank you again!) The trip to Key West took two days. Kept the hammer down, with only brief stops at Cracker Barrel parking lots and truck stops for naps. As we rolled south we were surrounded by zillions of Québécois who clog I-95 traversing from Canada to Florida. Not big on flying apparently. Anyway, we pulled into Boyd's and set up in our campsite with the back end of the coach eight feet from the water's edge. Had a great time until the biker gangs started showing up for the Island-wide New Year's Eve bash. When our Harley riding neighbors, (Family motto: 'Beer—It's What's For Breakfast'), started partying hard 24/7, and playing the "Who's Got The Loudest Un-Muffled Motorcycle Engine Game", we decided it was time to move on.

"What about the Mayor's Moose?" Wendy asked.
"Oh, yeah," I replied. "I forgot that part."

Mayor Ellen Moyer, of the City of Annapolis, has a stuffed moose larger than a person that she received as a gift. Through interesting circumstances we ended up with 'Moose Moyer' as our companion on the trip to Florida. For the first couple days, this was cute. Wendy bought him giant sunglasses at 'South of the Border'. (Official Motto: 'Pedro Says Give Us Lots Of Your Money And We'll Give You Some Crap Made In China Designed To Look Like It Was Made In Mexico.')

Underway Moose Moyer rode in the driver's seat of our Toad, Wendy's little SUV, towed behind The Moose. In-port we transferred him to the driver's seat of the coach. We planned to take pictures of him for the Mayor from all of our stopping places, but after awhile, maneuvering this honkin' big stuffed animal in and out of the Moose sort of stopped being as fun as we had initially thought.

And that kind of sums up the Moose story. Overall, we took three major trips including Oshkosh for the EAA airshow, and Bouckville, N.Y. for antique shopping, as well as several week-end jaunts. Altogether, over 8,000 miles. Very glad we did it. Now on to something different.

Chapter 22

The House

After my breeze through the McMansions of Davidsonville, I wasn't sure if this was an idea I wanted to get behind. I was still in the exploring mode and decided to bring Wendy in on my scheming.

Wendy is the greatest wife. She is usually so willing to go along with my crazy ideas (like buying a twenty-year-old RV on Ebay), but even Wendy has her limits. Since I end up exploring many ideas that never go anywhere, Wendy and I have an agreement. When I first bring up a new idea—like buying a 1963 Autogyro (kind of like a Helicopter with no engine driving the rotor) and trying for the Absolute World Record for gyro distance—I have to tell her if this is something we are really going to do, or am I just exploring the concept. The code phrase for her not to get worried *yet* is, "I'm just talking trash."

By the way, I did take several Autogyro flying lessons and traveled to Paducah, Kentucky to check out the feasibility of setting the world record in an Air & Space 18a Autogyro. I never really moved beyond the trash talk phase on this one. There *are* reasons that autogyro technology never advanced beyond 1936 levels.

As I entered the trash-talk phase of the New House project, I told Wendy what I was thinking. She has always wanted to build a house, and after 13 years in our old home, we were ready to move on. A quick call to my airplane partner, Mike Baldwin, President of Baldwin Homes, established rough parameters of what he could build for us, and for what kind of budget. It seemed feasible, if we could find the right building lot.

When I got into real estate in 1988, I spent a lot of time pre-viewing property all over the region to learn the inventory and neighborhoods. One property that had just been subdivided in the early 80's into two-acre lots was on Maynadier Creek off the Severn River, about half way to Annapolis from our old house. As a brand new agent, I remember trudging up to the top of a 67 foot knoll, on a small peninsula, and admiring the water view on three sides. What a great place to site a home.

Flash forward to January, 2003. I asked around the office to see if anybody knew of any new lots coming available that Wendy and I could look at. It turned out that the little knoll was back on the market and the price had just been slashed down into our range. The reason for the price drop—all permits, variances, and permission to build from Anne Arundel County Planning and Zoning had just expired. No guarantee that the county would let the buyer build anything. Sold strictly as-is.

Well, to make a long story short, we took a gamble on the permit issues, bought the lot, and started meeting with Mike's architect, Ash Roshan, to design the house. The building envelope and set-backs on our little knoll determined the shape of the house—an 'L'. Wendy and I defined the main elements of the house and drew up our thoughts of where they should be in relation to each other. Here is the design we gave Ash in our first design meeting.

Architects are like artists. If you like modern art, don't go to Rembrandt, and vice versa. We like traditional, but with a creative flair. Ash Roshan is truly a Grand Master at his craft. Fun to work with, and brilliantly creative, the process of watching Ash convert our little sketch into something that Mike could build has been a wonderful life experience. He took our ideas as a starting point and ran from there. He got further than our minds could have believed possible. His design is wonderful, and Wendy and I can't sing his praises loud enough. We'll just let his work—our house—stand on it's own.

When we were in our initial design meeting, Wendy, Ash, Mike and I talked through the important aspects of designing a house for the way we live. As we got to the end, I had a hidden agenda item I needed to bring up.

"There is just one other thing we'd like in the house, Ash," I said. "I probably watched too much *Wonderful World of Disney* growing up, but I want some secret passageways."

Mike's eyes rolled up in to his head at yet another crazy idea from me. Ash, on the other hand, was intrigued. "Sure! No problem," Ash said. "Like in that movie, *Panic Room*."

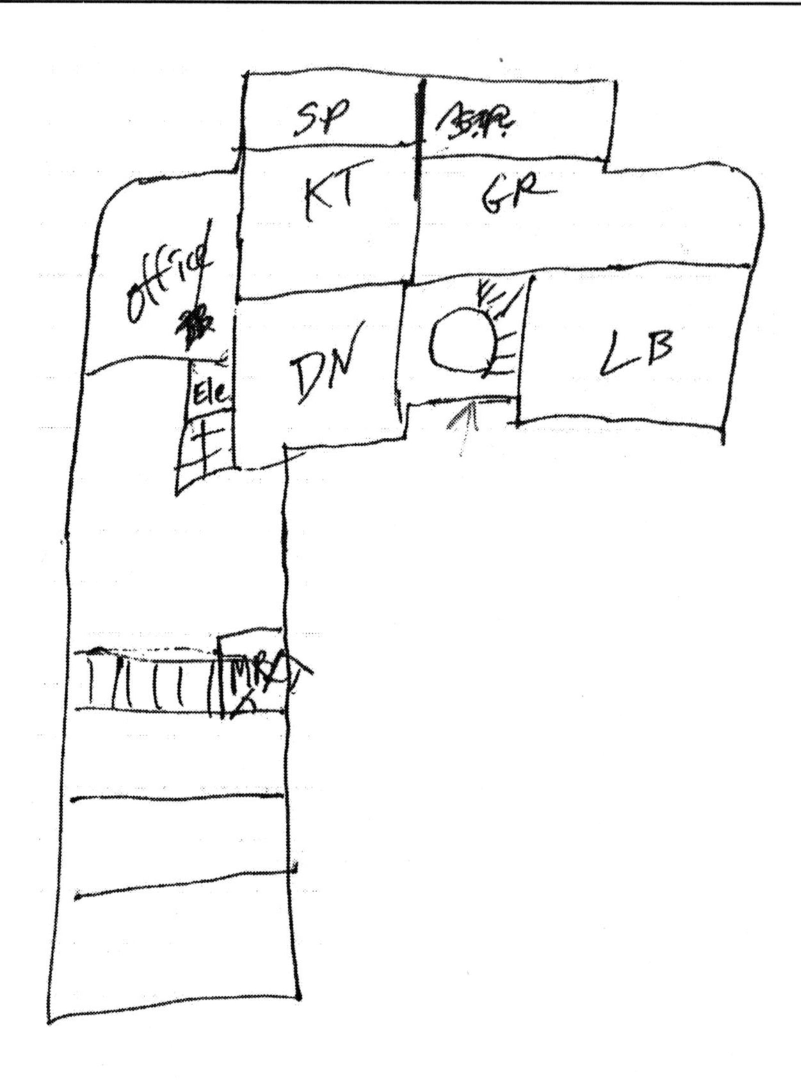

Mike's eyes rolled back down into view. After a brief pause, "Yeah, we can do a panic room," he confirmed. Panic Rooms are in vogue. Secret passageways are still a little out there, apparently.

Ash and I eventually cooked up a three-story spiral staircase that leads to a room hidden behind a mirror (I love one-way glass!). There may even be a few more secret passages in the house, but if I keep talking about them, they won't be very secret. When you come to visit, you have to find them yourself, but to give you a little bit of help, here is the actual blueprint of the main entrance to the spiral staircase that leads to one of our secret rooms. Good luck finding it!

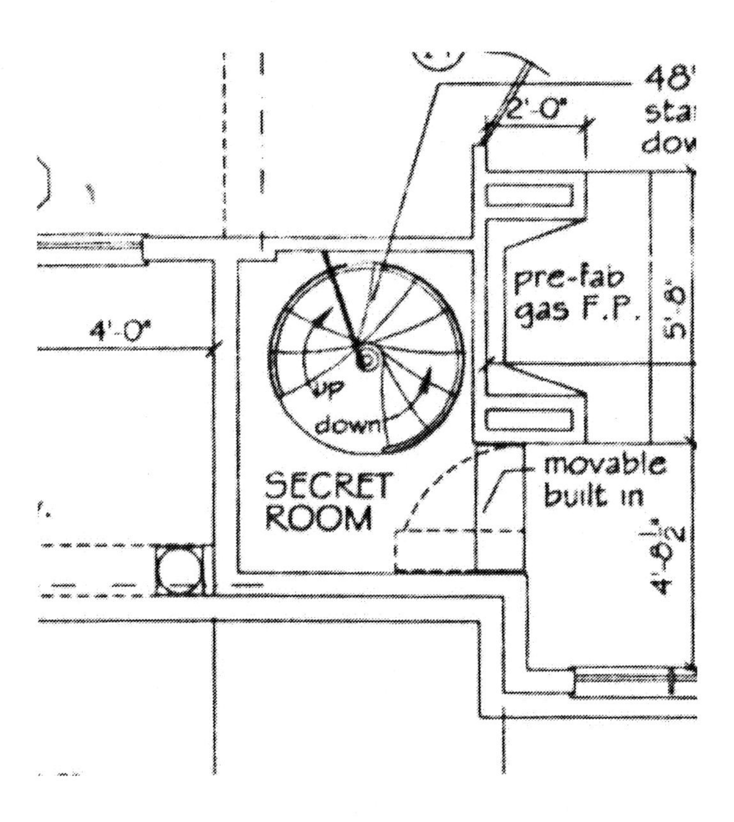

Oh, and for the rest of the story, we put our old house on the market in the spring. Sold it to the first family that saw it, closed in eight weeks and moved into a 1935 Cape Cod rental a few miles away from our old house. With luck we will be in to the new place by Memorial Day, 2005.

"Don't forget the Dock Gnomes," Wendy said.

"Coming up."

Chapter 23

Gnomes

GNOMES:

When we moved into our rental house, on the banks of the Magothy River, we cruised the neighborhood shoreline in our kayaks and found something new to us. Most of the homes had beautifully manicured lawns. That wasn't a surprise. The new part was that many of the homes had Dock Gnomes. Little Gnomes fishing off piers. Some sitting on benches. Others dressed like New England fishermen and light house keepers (complete with lighthouse). The record we found was fourteen Gnomes in one yard.

We were feeling a bit self-conscious at the lack of our own Dock Gnome, when much to our surprise, in the local grocery store, we found a large selection of Gnomes in the peanut butter aisle. Wendy let me select one with the latest in Gnome technology—a photovoltaic sensor that activates a light that emits a flickering glow from a lantern held aloft by the Gnome. Looks exactly like the light from a candle. We blend in now.

FAMILY:

To sum it up, we are all getting older.

In February, we attended a Memorial for my brother Russ in California. He loved to run in the hills about Oakland and wanted his ashes spread in the trees alongside the running trail. Afterward we all shared thoughts about what he meant to us in a very touching family gathering. Our Dad, Russell, Sr. and I committed at the memorial to get Russ' golf novel, ***Murder at Pebble Beach***, published. It is slated to come out right around the first of the year from iUniverse Publishing, so if you go to Amazon.com in January, search for the title. It is being released in both hardcover and paperback. Although I am slightly biased, I think it is a very good read.

My sister Jennifer had put together a "Roots" type family trip of discovery for the summer. Our mother, Ellen, is English. Jennifer, Andrew and I, with our families, wanted to go back to England with Ellen and Russell and get her to take us around and show us her favorite 'bits'. We planned out the trip with the California agent of a small English tour company that would be driving us around in our own little coach. Unfortunately, two things happened. First, my father, Russell went into the hospital in May. He was out of the hospital within a week, but the doctor restricted him from flying so he had to drop out. Ellen couldn't leave him alone, so she was out. With our tour guide/mother out, my brother Andrew decided to drop. But Wendy and I, with Jennifer, John and their daughter Sienna, decided to press on regardless and make the trip.

The second problem was with our itinerary. Planning in California, when you look at a map and see that Cheddar Gorge is only seven eighths of an inch away from Bath, it seems logical to drive back and forth between them on the same day. It wasn't the map scale that was flawed—the distance was under 25 miles. The problem is that, other than major motorways, English roads are direct descendants of ox cart tracks from the middle-ages or earlier. If the road is straight, the Romans built it. Unfortunately, the Romans didn't spend much time where we were. So, for a week, we wove our way around narrow roads in a thirteen-passenger mini-bus, with brief stops for a tour of a stately home or English Tea (a cup of the drink, plus a scone with clotted cream and jam to eat.). It was fun despite the time spent in the bus, and the highlight of the trip for us was the last week-end with my mother's sister, Violet, and my cousin Diane and her family. We even got a tour of Gnome Magic with thousands of the little buggers, including an Arnold Schwarzenegger look-alike.

Just before we left for England, Wendy's brother-in-law, Richard, lost his mother to cancer. The family had just moved her into a new condo thinking the disease would take months or even years to progress, not just days. Their family all convened on Winter Haven, Florida for the funeral, just as we departed to fly across the Atlantic.

After the funeral, as the family made their way back home to various points on the East Coast, in the middle of the afternoon, on a sunny day, two exits from her home in Georgia, Richard's sister, Michelle, was killed in a freak one-car accident. Forty-nine years old, and gone in an instant. Her cousin, Debbie was critically injured and remained in a coma for weeks before coming around. There is probably a life lesson here, but we are all still too stunned at the tragedy to process it.

I didn't meet Michelle and Debbie for my first fifteen years in the Weeks/Barton family, but had the pleasure of vacationing with them last year, including taking Michelle flying with her two children. Be thankful for what we get out of life, I guess. We still don't understand.

ETCETRA:

For my tenth, eleventh and twelfth grades I went to High School in High Wycombe, England. London Central is a DoD Dependant's school for Army/Navy/Air Force brats. We had a Reunion in Las Vegas in September and it was the first time I had seen these people in 30 years. It was dramatically more fun than I expected, and I'm really looking forward to spending more time with the friends of my youth at the next reunion in 2005.

Wendy has become quite an accomplished Ebay sniper. It started with a quest at antique shows for the last couple years. She has been on the hunt to find Anchor Hocking frosted 'dot' glasses, like the ones she drank from in her youth in the early 60's in Rochester, New York. Tall frosted tumblers with big polka-dots in red, green, black and blue. Despite countless hours searching through New England antique shops, and chasing leads down blind canyons searching for this elusive piece of Kennedy-era Americana, she only came up with one dot glass in the last two years.

Then she discovered Ebay.

At first, Wendy would get excited and put a bid in when the Dot Glass first appeared for auction. This precipitated a run-up in prices as she battled with other bidders, and when she got beat out over and over at the final bell, she wondered what was happening.

Other than the Moose, I've never bought on Ebay so I wasn't much help. She did some research and found out she had been 'sniped'. Basically, as I understand it, a sniper waits until the last 30 seconds of the auction and throws in a huge proxy bid. The computer at Ebay, automatically bids against all newcomers for you, going up fifty cents at a time until you have bested your competition. The theory on sniping is that, with only 30 seconds to react to your last minute bid, the poor chump who was the previous high bidder doesn't have time to wake up to the new situation, and the auction times out before they get their act together.

Since she learned how to play the Ebay game, Wendy hasn't lost yet! We are now drowning in a couple dozen dot glasses, and Wendy is culling the herd, intending to put the rejects that are faded, or surplus for some reason, back into the Ebay pool. If you need any Ebay bidding advice—or Dot glasses—call Wendy.

I turned to Wendy as I finished writing this letter. "I'm not happy with this one. It has less zing than last year's letter, which had less pop then the year before. I'm on the slippery slope to boredom. We'll be mailing out fruit cake next."

"Well," Wendy replied. "It is a little less exciting, but that might be because, once again, this year nobody tried to kill us. Besides, the gag is in the presentation. The blueprint carries the letter."

"Great. I'm reduced to writing prop comedy."

"Hey, this is probably the first and last BluePrint® Holiday Letter that will ever get produced. Didn't you say you had to get our grading engineers to produce this as one of the final jobs before they shipped their BluePrint® machine off to a museum?"

"I did say that, and while it might be a slight embellishment, the truth is that black and white Xerox copiers have just about completely replaced BluePrint® machines in the building trades. This letter belongs in a museum."

"Don't get carried away. It's not that good."

<u>Invitation:</u>

We are having a:

'Muddy Boots Open House'
from
1–5 pm
on
Sunday, January 2nd, 2005

at our house under construction. Dress warm—No heat yet! Wear shoes you don't mind getting muddy—it is a construction site. Hope to see you there! I'm out of inches! Got to go...

Christmas—2005

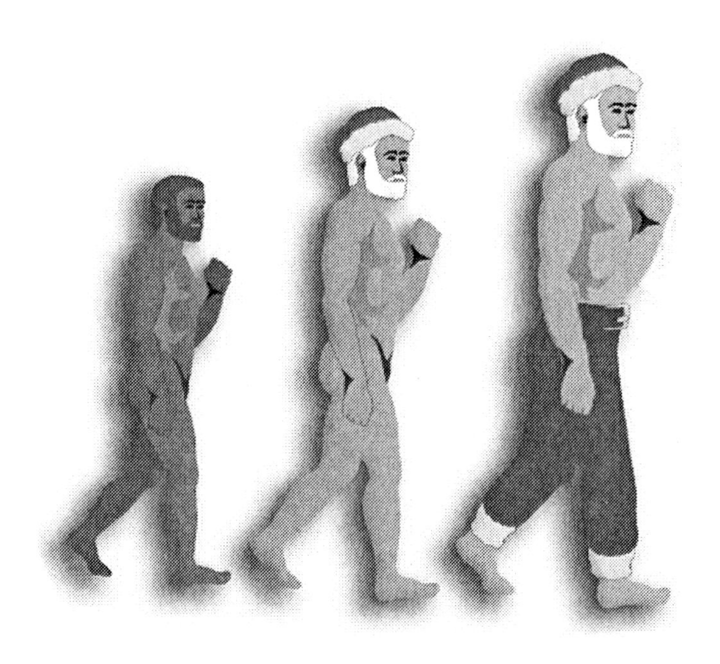

Chapter 24

Muddy Boots Open House

Hi, there. Are you still reading, or did you flip right to this spot to get caught up with the latest adventures of Jon & Wendy. If you waded through the pages of our past to get here, thanks for hanging in there. Statistically you are one out of six who did it that way. According to something I think I may have actually read somewhere, less than 15% of books that are sold in stores are ever read by anybody. If you made it here by reading, we salute you!

Looking back, that first letter did read a bit like a diary. However when one of my neighbors, Chris Wood, said he quit taking flying lessons after reading about our little excitement in the clouds over Kalamazoo it did give me pause. I was conflicted. Proud that my writing was strong enough to influence somebody's behavior, but disappointed that I had turned somebody away from the great hobby of flying.

But enough about ancient history. Let's get going with our 2005: Year in Review.

Our year kicked off for us on a very cold Sunday. January 2nd, the day of the "Muddy Boots Open House". We had sent out over 150 **BluePrint®** Xmas Letter/Invitations to family and friends all over the globe: Europe, Asia, California, Hawaii, the Midwest and the Middle East (Israel), and even a few locally. (While that may sound like a lot, our friend, Jenny Pruitt in Atlanta papers the globe with over 1,600 inspirational holiday letters annually!)

Anyway, when the day dawned with a bleak gray overcast, and temperatures struggling to get up into the 40's, we didn't know what to expect for a turnout.

"The caterer wants the final headcount," Wendy said, turning to me with the phone in hand.

I looked over our Christmas Card List. Backing out the ones from distant lands, I took a stab at a guess.

"Tell them to plan on forty. We may only have twenty but if that's the case we can subsist on the leftovers for a week or two."

I was banking on my theory that caterers always overstock and if people came late, they probably wouldn't expect too much in the food department anyway. With visitors due within two hours, I jumped in the car and headed off to a wholesale liquor mart to stock up. My writer friends were coming and that meant I needed wine, and lots of it.

When I arrived at Osprey Point, Wendy and the caterer were already in the midst of setting up food, displays, and room signs. The house was just an empty structure at the framing stage, with exterior walls and windows in place keeping out most of the wind, and two by four stud walls defining the rooms. It was retaining the night cold. A propane heater sitting in the middle of the concrete slab of the basement floor was roaring like a jet fighter. The heat shooting out the end of the industrial heater was intense for a distance of six feet, but farther away then that, the cold air pouring in from outside through the gap that would one day hold our front door mixed with this propane heat and diluted the heat plume down to barely warmer than the outside air temperature. I hoped everyone would dress appropriately.

"Do you have a spackle bucket?" The caterer asked.

"We don't even have drywall yet. I doubt there is any spackle around here," I replied.

"That's okay. I brought four of my own. It would have been nice to have a couple more but this will do. I'm going to stick some dead twigs in the spackle for the centerpiece. Kind of a Muddy Boots construction theme."

Donna, the catering manager from Graul's Supermarket, a local Annapolis institution, showed me the rest of the party décor. She was using paint roller trays for cheese platters. In our future great room, chest high cocktail tables were covered with brown paper topped with more spackling bucket flower arrangements. Sterno fires kept the Maryland Crab Soup warm, while the environment chilled the beer. We were ready for company by the time our first guest arrived.

"Wendy, I'm going to start *Top Gun*," I said as I headed down the back staircase to the basement. It would be months before the front staircase railing was installed, and for now the only safe way up and down was the back stairs. Luckily, without walls in place, I could just cut between the studs in the dining room wall and take a short cut.

Down in the basement, in the approximate location where the movie theater would eventually go, I hung a sheet from the ceiling and placed four plastic deck chairs in the approximate location of the future rows of seats. Running a power cable in from a generator outside, I turned on the two strings of bare light bulbs I had hung throughout the lower level for lighting, and powered up the LCD projector. Unfortunately, without all the theater walls in place the ambient light streaming in the windows washed out the picture, and the propane heater's roar drowned out the soundtrack, but at least the essence of what would eventually fill this end of the basement was apparent to those who would venture down this far.

At noon our guests started to arrive. With labels in each room identifying the ultimate use of the space, people were able to take their own self-guided tours, warmed by hot soup or a glass of wine.

Like many people, we have old, old friends on our Christmas Card List who we haven't seen in years. Good friends from our youth that time and distance have prevented us from seeing face-to-face, but who we still harbor hopes of getting to spend quality time with, if not now, perhaps when life slows down a bit at some ill-defined point in the future. We keep exchanging Xmas Letters, staying somewhat in touch, and annually recommit to get together sometime "very soon."

As the guests started to arrive, to our pleasant surprise, many of these old dear friends were in the herd. Walking up the muddy drive leading to our house under construction we spotted Carol and Reid and their daughters, Olivia and Lillian. Hadn't seen them since before Lillian was born, and she's now a teenager! Then came Scott and Chris Wilson, followed by John Clifford, and on and on. A clump of famous writers from the Washington-Baltimore-Annapolis area showed up. These creative types are self-entertaining and the snippets of conversation I shared with them grew wittier by the second as the wine flowed out of our future cellar and down their gullets.

It was a perfect way to start the New Year with many of our best friends in life. As the sun set, the sterno died down, and the generator ran out of gas the party wound down naturally. It was an auspicious start to the new year.

January started on such a high, but would it stay that way? We were about to find out.

Chapter 25

Pauline

"There is a problem with the gills on your cat," the hippie veterinarian surgeon said as he languorously slid down the wall in the examining room and squatted in a heap on the floor. His fine brown hair hanging down to the middle of his back appeared to be frequently brushed, but with nothing tying it back it was swishing all over the place. Keeping one hand in constant motion to corral the hair, the doctor was explaining our little Pauline's medical predicament.

"I think we need to operate and take them out," he said, as his hand flipped the hair up off of one ear. I hadn't seen hair in motion like this since 9th grade. I kept my eye on the show as I peppered the doc with questions.

"Cats have gills? I didn't even think they liked the water," I replied.

"Well, they aren't actual gills, but more like the evolutionary leftovers from when they might have been water breathers," he tried to explain. "Cats are living much longer these days then they used to and we are seeing new ailments crop up that we've never seen before. She's just getting to be an old girl. These growths we are seeing might be something left over from when the embryo was developing. Normally they sprout gill-like membranes at one point in gestation and then these gills get re-absorbed and mutated into other organs as the embryo evolves into a cat and one theory is that the biological clock sets them off again to reappear."

It sounded like he was making stuff up. The more he talked, the more he squirmed around, sliding up and down the wall like he was one of his dog patients trying to scratch his back on a fence post. Only difference really is that this dog drives a BMW and he was looking for a few months of payments from us for the surgery. But as he talked on, he actually started to sound like he knew what he was talking about, and that he truly liked and cared about our the health and comfort of our little Pauline. He had come highly recommended and so we listened.

"It's up to you, but if she was my kitty, I would do the surgery. It's not uncommon or difficult and she should recover fine. But, she is an old girl and we don't know how much time she has left. The surgery will make her time remaining more comfortable."

Pauline, our little black kitty had come to us right after we got married. We were living in Key West at the time and decided that we needed a playmate for Hemingway. For sixteen years, Pauline shared our home, and allowed us to share her bed. While our other animals seemed to need periodic vet visits for some ailment or other, Pauline never got sick, right up until this episode. We could tell she was in quite some discomfort with these lumps on her neck and if removing these gill bits would make her better we were all for it.

Sadly, the operation didn't have permanent results and within a few months she was letting us know it was time to go join Hemingway and Keesha up at the Rainbow Bridge. Uncomplaining to the end, we were very sad she would never get to experience the cat doors we were having built into the new house for her and Leo. They aren't doors to the outside, but little doors that would allow cat-sized animals to get into various rooms, while dog-sized objects would be locked out.

It was a somber household for several weeks after Pauline left us. Then the Chinese and Norwegians entered our lives and stirred things up.

More accurately, I should say the Chinese and Norwegians entered Wendy's life and started stirring.

Chapter 26

The Tour de Clay

One of the enjoyable aspects of taking up an artsy kind of hobby like writing has been the creative souls we have gotten to know. While Wendy was back in the Navy Reserves, spending her weekends eating MREs, wearing camouflage BDUs and combat boots, and filling up the Republican side of our dance card, I was getting in touch with our liberal side by bring home writer friends to balance out our social life. Leveraging off of her military contracting experience, six years ago Wendy got hired to be Purchasing Coordinator for Anne Arundel Community College. Since then, her professional focus has evolved from purchasing weapon systems to contracting for classroom buildings.

As the College has grown, so have the building projects, and Wendy has found herself consumed with the job. None of these building projects prepared her for the "Tour de Clay". Eight hundred and seventy eight artists, one hundred and sixty exhibitions, the world's biggest ceramic art display, and right here in Maryland with the College hosting part of the show. Now it was Wendy's turn to mingle with artists.

Two years in the preparation, the College had decided that their part of the exhibition would be to host a collection of Norwegian clay sculpture that was on a multi-year world tour. As the contracting officer for the College, it became Wendy's job to contract for shipping of the Norwegian ceramics from their last exhibition at a museum in the People's Republic of China, half-way around the world to the Arnold campus.

Everything was going fine. The arrangements were made with the international shippers for loading in Shanghai. A contract was placed with a container ship to deliver the goods in time for the grand opening. Negotiations were made to engage a shipping agent on the Baltimore end to coordinate between customs and the bonded warehouse at the port. Everything was tracking along on schedule until Wendy noticed a little remark, buried on the shipping manifest.

"Contents: Norwegian artwork and assorted other Chinese stuff?" Wendy repeated into the phone to the shipping agent. "What 'stuff'?"

"No problem," the shipping agent in Shanghai said over the long distance phone line. "We do this all the time. We just added a few extra things to the container to make it a full load and after you sign for the shipment with U.S. Customs, someone will drop by to pick up the other goods."

"Other goods?" Wendy still wasn't understanding. "The College paid for the entire container. There aren't supposed to be any other goods."

"Don't worry," the agent reassured her. "You will be reimbursed for shipping the other stuff."

"We don't care about that. What exactly is the other stuff you expect us to sign for?"

"Miscellaneous goods. Things made in China. I don't really know what was in the boxes."

"Let me get this straight," Wendy replied. "The College paid for an entire container. But now, unbeknownst to us, there are other goods in the container. But nobody knows what those boxes contain. You are telling me that we can't get our container out of bonded warehouse at the port unless the College accepts the entire shipment?"

"Exactly," the elated shipping agent said over the phone in very broken English, but with a heavy New York accent. "You've got it. Just sign please."

"I'll get back to you," Wendy said, ringing off to do some research.

After many calls to the attorney on retainer to the College, the shipping agent at the bonded warehouse in Baltimore, the Norwegians who were coordinating the exhibition of their clays, and back to China, it was decided that all she needed to do was get some clarity around what was in the extra boxes.

A middle of the night phone call, with a translator, was planned to the shippers in Shanghai.

"It's Chinese New Year," the shipper patiently explained. "Everybody gone."

"Okay," Wendy said. "We'll call back tomorrow after the holiday."

"No. Everybody gone for two weeks."

"Everybody?" Wendy asked.

"Yes."

Everyone in China is gone? Wendy tried to understand what she was being told. *This has to be a joke.*

"You can't reach anybody who knows what went into our container."

"Everybody gone. Entire country goes on holiday for Chinese New Year. Two weeks," The shipper explained. "Maybe we'll find out then."

Wendy was in a pickle. The opening night VIP reception with the Consul General of the United Nations delegation from Norway, was scheduled for mid-March. She couldn't wait for the holiday to end. Extensive negotiations with lawyers, the Norwegians, the Baltimore shipping agent and the Chinese had the container alternating between being shipped back to China, sent on to Norway unopened, or left in bonded storage to rot, at the expense of the College of course. Nobody—not the Norwegians, the Chinese or the College were willing to sign and accept the entire shipment without an accurate shipping manifest.

After much hullabaloo over a period of several weeks, Wendy ultimately sorted out the dilemma with the help of a Chinese-American business professor faculty member and the College lawyer and the container was delivered literally in the nick of time. Much to her relief, Customs and DEA agents didn't leap out of the bushes when the container doors were opened, revealing the ceramics and a few innocuous boxes of Chinese tee-shirts.

In addition to getting referenced in an article in the local newspaper, the *Evening Capital* about solving the shipping tribulations, Wendy received an invitation for us to attend the opening night VIP reception with the Consul General, a kindly grandmother type who reminded me of my own Norwegian grandmother.

The clay object d'art were very interesting, but for me, they sort of lacked sizzle. My life at this stage was all about sizzle, and lots of it. I was afraid I was turning into a sizzle junkie.

Chapter 27

Sizzle Points

When Wendy and I embarked on our adventure to build a house, we quickly came to understand that we were either going to absolutely love this new house, or we were going to find it uncomfortably big and would want to sell it quickly and move back down to something of a more familiar size.

Several years ago, old Navy friends from Key West, Tony and Carole Martonosi decided to move up to a big house. We received their change of address but didn't have time to get out to St. Louis to see the new home before we received another change of address as they moved back down to something smaller. We never got the full story, but as we embarked on our building project, four out of five friends with large homes were telling us, "Don't make it too big."

Now what exactly is the definition of "too big?"

When we bought the lot, the topography and previous variances dictated the foot print. The previous owner wanted to build a 9,300 square-foot French Chateau. We knew that wasn't our style, and as we worked with the architect and builder, our plans evolved into a smaller Cape Cod.

But even with the house scaled down, we weren't sure if we would feel comfortable or out of place in a home considerable bigger than the one we had lived in for thirteen years in Severna Park. If it wasn't right for us, we wanted to make sure it was very marketable so we could bail out quick. That is when I remembered a lesson I had learned doing new homes marketing up in Baltimore in the 90's. Sizzle points.

It's almost a cliché in sales that while people want to eat a steak, they buy for the sizzle. If we were one of many houses on the market, we needed to have tons of sizzle so ours would stand out from the pack and sell quickly. The ultimate sizzle point I had encountered in my travels was in a model home north of Baltimore. The decorator had convinced the builder to finish off a little pocket of space under the eaves, next to a roof gable and had decorated this little four-foot tall cubby-hole with foam rocks lining the walls. It looked just like a cave. Then an entrance hole was cut into one of the kid bedrooms to access the "cave". Every family that came into that model home with small children ended up spending lots of time in the sales trap as they tried unsuccessfully to pry their kids out of the cave. When the family ultimately left our model to drive around and look at our competition in other new home communities, we just knew that the kids, juiced up from the plentiful candy bowls we had also strategically scattered around our model, were bouncing around the back seat of the car lobbying hard for their parents to buy them a house with a cave in their bedroom. That is truly the power of sizzle.

Wendy and I evaluated our target market. Moving into a community of two-acre lots, and with sparse development on this side of the river, most of our neighbors are empty nesters. A first floor master bedroom would be a hot selling point for the grandparent types who might be our future target buyers. The only problem with first floor master suites is that they sacrifice a lot of the floor area on the first level. Smaller kitchens, family rooms, dining rooms, and other living spaces are the inevitable result. I never liked the trade-off myself. Then I remembered something.

We have friends in Northern Virginia, Mark & Jackie Graham, who told us years ago about somebody they knew who was building a huge mansion in Great Falls. In the 18 years that passed, the only thing I remember from the description of this wonderful house is that it had—an elevator.

Elevators are very rare in private homes in Anne Arundel County. If we installed an elevator, that would accomplish two things. First, we could put the master bedroom suite upstairs where we thought it belonged, without fear of scarring off any buyers. Second, how cool is that having our own elevator! Now that is sizzle—plus a little bit of steak thrown in.

The next sizzle point that seems trendy in modern homes is a Movie Theater. We had seen many of these in our travels while looking for design ideas. Any movie theater is cool, but a BIG movie theater is way cooler! We decided on a twenty-seat room, with three levels of seating. If you are going to have three levels, these days you just have to go with stadium seating. As one would expect, the screen is huge and detail previously missed in movies is very easy to see when blown up this large. For example, Tom Cruise's head is the size of a weather balloon in the *Top Gun* cockpit close-ups.

The next sizzle point we explored is a very controversial one in real estate circles. As a good real estate agent, I know that swimming pools are totally neutral when it comes to adding value to a house. Some people love them. Some hate them. For the folks who hate them, as agents we always say not to worry. It is very cheap to fill a pool in with dirt.

For therapeutic reasons, Wendy wanted an "Endless Pool". In one of those, a hydraulic motor circulates the water through ducts and creates a current, like a swiftly flowing river, that comes out of one end. You swim in the middle into the current, making one infinite "lap" of the pool, until you tire and drift to the back wall, or slide out of the current to either side and sit on the underwater bench. With a deep area to allow her to do water aerobics without touching the bottom, Wendy thought her needs to do zero-impact aerobics would be met with this solution. Due to the constraints of the site, and Wendy's desire to be able to use the pool year-round, we decided to put the pool in its own room in the basement. So, whether our mythical future buyer likes pools or not, I still think it is a little bit of a sizzle point to have an indoor pool, albeit a small one.

Our next sizzle point revolved around sitting outside at night. In Maryland that is a good way to attract bugs. We decided early on that we wanted a screen porch incorporated into the design of the house. Our good friend, stock broker Mike Stack, and his wife had just finished building a house north of Baltimore. Previewing our construction project, Mike shared with us that the coolest thing he did in his house was to put in a "Brewmaster" ceiling fan. It sounded perfect for our screen porch. The "Brewmaster" has a motor mounted to the ceiling near the wall, while the fan blades are mounted in two locations out near the center of the room. As the motor turns, it revolves a double sheaved pulley. Leather belts lead through these sheaves, and run out twelve feet to the fan blade assembly. At the top of this assembly there is another pulley near the ceiling connected to a shaft that runs down to the fan. The belts lead around this second pulley and back toward the motor. When you turn on the fan, the motor starts turning, pulling the belts and by their traveling through the pulleys the fan blades turn. You may have seen something similar in bars—hence the name "The Brewmaster".

The leather belts are held together with rivets. It is, excuse the term, riveting to watch these rivets make their laps between motor and fan blade, and back to motor, in an unending progression. Some times, if you listen carefully, when the rivets hit the pulley they make a faint clattering noise of metal-on-metal. The two belts obviously turn at the same speed, but with the distance between motor and the two separate blade assemblies being slightly unequal, one set of rivets rotates with a barely perceptible shorter lap-time. I don't think it is just me, as other guys who have visited have also found countless hours of enjoyment sitting back, drinking a beer, watching to see which set of rivets are actually gaining on the other.

Rounding out the sizzle on the screen porch, we installed a stainless steel gas fireplace in the corner to give us some heat on cool fall evenings.

For the final sizzle point, we chose something out of the ordinary. It actually may even be a bit too unusual to generate true sizzle, but it does put a smile on people's faces when they discover it. Our final addition involves secret passageways, a hidden three-story spiral staircase leading to a concrete and rebar lined panic room with a disguised one-way mirror allowing those in the know to keep an eye on people in the house without their knowing that they are being watched.

I'm not telling you any more about the secret passageways. You have to find it all yourself. But maybe I will include a couple clues in the next chapter or two.

Chapter 28

Woodstock For Capitalists

In my job as President of Champion Realty, I'm fortunate to get to spend time every three months with a truly great group of people. Our regional real estate company executives have quarterly CEO meetings, held in conjunction with our Board of Directors meetings. Being an affiliate of Berkshire Hathaway, periodically these meetings are timed to coincide with events attended by Warren Buffett, the internationally famous investor and head of our ultimate parent company, Berkshire Hathaway.

This year's second quarter meeting was done in conjunction with the Berkshire Hathaway annual meeting in Omaha, Nebraska. While most CEOs dread this annual opportunity for shareholders to pepper them with questions, Warren Buffett actually relishes it, making a week-end long spectacle out of the ordeal. In his words, he calls it "Woodstock for Capitalists."

With some excitement at being invited to mingle with the business greats of our nation, I arrived in Omaha in time for dinner on the Wednesday before the big Saturday shareholder meeting. I dropped my bags in the hotel across from the Qwest Center and jumped in a van with some of the other leadership of HomeServices of America for the ride to a trendy restaurant in the refurbished downtown core of Omaha. When I walked in the front door, the bar area of the restaurant was packed with the ubiquitous young professional crowd found in any city in America. I was directed to follow the herd of our blue-suited executives back through the crush to the entrance of a private dining room. We turned left and passed through a door into a darkened room. The far end of the room was wall to ceiling glass, a plate glass window looking out on the brightly sunlit street. The glare coming in the window silhouetted a sea of suits in front of me, but with no light from the darkened room behind me I couldn't make out faces until I was right on top of them. I stepped forward into the glare.

"Hey, Jon. Great to see you." A hand reached out of the gloom and shook my hand.

"Oh," I exclaimed in surprise, my hand to my forehead shielding my eyes from the bright glare. "Brad. I didn't recognize you." My eyes were struggling as my pupils dilated and contracted in rapid succession as my gaze passed from light to dark to light again. The push of more executives coming in behind me propelled me forward into the room, past Brad DeVries, the CEO of our Kentucky company. I bumped into the next person ahead of me.

"Ron!" I said, perhaps louder than I should. I had popped through the gloom and was suddenly thrust face-to-face with our CEO, Ron Peltier.

"Jon. I see you made it...Good flight?...Glad you're here...Keep moving...More people right behind you." Ron, a former hockey player and Captain of the University of Minnesota Golden Gophers pirouetted me around like I was on figure skates, and launched me ten feet further into the room, right into a one-on-one, face-to-face, *mano-a-mano*, *tête-à-tête* with...

W.B.

Yikes!

"Mr. Buffett," I said, re-introducing myself to the spry business man sipping a Cherry Coke in front of me. He looked like he was 80% of his chronological age of 74 and was feeding himself like he was 10% of it. I guess if you are the second richest man in the world you don't have to eat your peas if you don't want to. Cherry Coke was his drink, and not the diet kind either. My mouth kicked into gear with banal greetings. "Blah, blah, blah."

I hadn't prepped and didn't have a thing intelligent to say. I knew I was coming to Omaha, and would get to see WB on stage at the annual meeting, but I thought I would be buried in the crowd with the other 24,000 shareholders and managers attending the highlight of the Omaha social season. I'd met him twice before so this wasn't the big deal it was the first time but nobody told me that we would be having dinner and that I would get some solo face time with the man himself. I knew I needed to stop stammering and start sounding like an executive as my mind tried to kick my butt into gear. *Think fast, monkey boy!*

"So, are you all set for the Annual meeting on Saturday?" I said. "Have you been practicing your remarks in front of the bathroom mirror." I was so proud of my cleverness on short notice. Talking like a peer. Comparing notes on giving speeches to the masses although my typical crowd of 50-200 was less than the security force laid in for his big speech coming up on Saturday.

"No, no. I don't practice," Mr. Buffett replied, telling me what every book on Berkshire Hathaway clearly stated in Chapter One. He was famous, renown, notorious for just sitting up on stage at these annual meeting with his partner, Charlie Munger, for six hours straight. They would sit and eat See's Candy, drink Coke and munch on other Berkshire products while taking any and all questions from the audience. No limits. No restrictions. He is a well-known advocate for transparency in corporate governance and would answer any question posed by any shareholder. I probably should have known that fact, but he was kind in explaining it all to me. "I don't rehearse anything. I don't have any prepared remarks. I just take the questions as they come."

We chatted for a couple minutes about the events of the week ahead and then the influx of the rest of our management team behind me shunted me on to the next person in the informal receiving line—Walter Scott, the only other septuagenarian multi-billionaire I happen to know. Mr. Scott is a member of the Berkshire Hathaway Board and had joined us for dinner the last time we met with Warren Buffett. Where Wendy and I have a Golden Retriever and a cat for pets, Mr. Scott has a team of Clydesdale Draft Horses. We have a boat. He has a yacht larger than the last warship I served on in the United States Navy. It's all just a matter of scale.

After dinner it was back to the hotel, and early to bed. We had a full agenda of meetings scheduled for the next day.

After our meetings ended on Thursday, about half our management team headed for home. I elected to stick around and work from my Omaha hotel room on Friday, and experience the excitement of the Berkshire annual meeting at dawn on Saturday.

Friday night, after dinner, I was in the lobby bar of the Omaha Hilton hotel, having a nightcap with several other HomeServices types, when Bob Moline, CEO of our Lincoln, Nebraska company looked over my shoulder and said, "There goes Bill Gates."

My head snapped around like Rosemary in *Rosemary's Baby*, trying to get a glimpse of "Number One"—the only guy on the planet richer than our boss.

In the distance, like a stream swallowing a rock, the crowd was closing back around a small character, blocking him from view. He appeared to be cruising past the bar at a quick clip, scanning the crowd for somebody. In a flash he was around the corner and out of sight. I had barely seen him.

I leapt up and sprinted around to the back side of the bar, floating in the middle of the hotel lobby. If he was heading up to his room in the hotel, he'd have to circle back and I could intercept him there. A phalanx of other geeks had the same idea as me, and launched themselves out of their bar stools and chairs and headed for the exact same spot I was aiming for, trying to head him off at the pass. We careened around the corner like paparazzi, but without cameras, and skidded to a stop on the slick marble floor.

There he was! Walking right towards us, wife Melinda a scant half-step behind.

My first thought was, *He's short.*

Like dogs chasing cars, none of us had figured out what we would do if we actually caught up with the founder of Microsoft. He kept walking towards us, and silently, almost reverently, we parted, letting Mr. & Mrs. Gates walk through without a word being exchanged by either side.

As the crowd melted back to their respective bar stools, we watched from a distance as Bill and Melinda headed for the elevator. In the morning he was going to be elected to the Berkshire Board of Directors, while we watched from the bleachers.

Back at the bar, Bob Moline reached across the table and handed me the golden ticket. "Here you go, Jon. Take my 'Event Staff' badge. It will get you in to the Qwest Center before it opens at 7:00am."

"Are you sure?" I asked. I already had a 'Shareholder' badge that would get me in for the annual meeting, but the Event Staff got special privileges. Early access and a free lunch being two of the biggest.

"This thing is bigger than a rock concert. The shareholders start lining up before four in the morning tomorrow to get in but the doors don't open until seven. With this badge you can get in to help set up our booth and check things out before the crowds show up. By the time they open, there will be over five thousand people in line around the block and they start running for the best seats as soon as they get in. Go in early and experience the whole thing. I live in Lincoln. I've seen it all before. Just get over there early, like around six. Warren usually walks through the exhibit hall before they open the doors and has his picture taken with everybody."

I couldn't believe his generosity. The event staff badges were getting harder and harder to get, and only a handful of our group scored them.

I rolled out of bed at 5:30 am, showering and suiting up in HomeServices-logo business casual attire. Just after six, I exited the hotel and looked across the street at the orderly mob of shareholders. Thousands of them in the pre-dawn gloom, lined up down the block and around the corner as promised. TV crews were trolling the line, shooting little fluff bits to insert on CNN, FOX, CNBC and the local affiliates of the major networks when they aired this story of the day in the financial news.

With my golden ticket, I waltzed past the crowds and entered the Qwest Center, the huge multi-purpose arena that houses everything from Basketball to Rock Concerts. In the convention display area, all of the subsidiary companies of Berkshire Hathaway had exhibit space and the consumer companies had goods to sell at special bargain basement rates for shareholders only.

My first stop was at our booth. The real professionals in our marketing group had already set us up and so there was no work for me. After checking in I decided to take a quick tour of the other companies on the convention floor.

See's Candy had mounds of chocolate on display—for purchase. Clayton Manufactured Homes had brought an entire house into the convention hall and would be offering tours to shareholders. Mid-American Energy had a brand new truck with cherry picker to service power lines. Waxed and gleaming, with their logo prominently displayed, it was parked next to our booth where we had all of our different regional brand 'For Sale' signs. From ice cream (Dairy Queen) to cowboy boots, to carpet, to furniture, to diamonds, all the Berkshire Hathaway companies had gone to great lengths to impress the shareholders with the extent of Berkshire's holdings.

Over at the Ginzu Knife display (another Berkshire company), I was tempted by their extensive array of product being offered at deeply discounted prices. I had selected several packages of assorted Ginzu knives when I remembered that I had only brought carry-on luggage. If I tried to check in at the airport with a roll-on full of knives...

Reluctantly I put the knives back and headed to our booth to meet and greet shareholders for awhile before moving up to the arena floor to hear Warren and Charlie answer questions. There was one hot issue concerning a Department of Justice investigation into one of the insurance companies owned by Berkshire that had the crowd in a titter. How would Warren handle that question? We would soon find out.

The arena was set up for our rock concert. One end was filed with a stage, with screens suspended from the ceiling on either side of the stage. Directly in front, where the mosh pit might have been if it was going to be Jimmy instead of Warren Buffett up on stage, rows of plastic folding chairs were set up in a roped off and guarded area. The roped area was for the Board of Directors. Further back, the floor seats were for senior executives of the various divisions. Less senior executives and shareholders rounded out the crowd, filling every seat from the floor to the upper deck. Three thousand late-comers couldn't fit in so were shunted over to a ballroom atop the exhibit hall to watch the show on a huge projection screen.

My fellow HomeServices executives had staked out an area right off the floor. We were in the nearest section to the stage on the left, and as

Bill Gates showed up and entered the Board area we realized we probably had a better view of the dais than he did from his seat down on the floor. We certainly weren't any further away.

The meeting kicked off with an hour long comedy video. This year's effort was a spoof of *The Wizard of Oz*. Using product endorsement gags reminiscent of Mike Myer in *Wayne's World*, Mr. Buffett plugged most of the different divisions and substantial shareholdings of Berkshire. With cameos from some of his celebrity friends, including Arnold Schwarzenegger, and nephew Jimmy Buffett, the hour flew by. Then it was time for the live show.

The curtain parted and Warren and Charlie walked through and took their places, sitting front and center at a cloth-draped table. They each had a microphone on a short stand at their seat, a six-pack of Cherry Coke iced down within reach, and boxes of See's candy and peanut brittle where a lesser CEO might have wanted notes to refer to during the questioning. Clearly their answers were all going to be off the top of their head.

After settling in, Warren kicked off the show, tapping the end of his microphone to see if it was on, and doing his volume check of the PA system.

"One billion, two billion, three billion. Can everybody hear me?" Warren said to the crowd.

Start off light when you know a zinger is coming. He is a master of public speaking and was in his element. I guess when you are the second richest guy on the planet, you don't really need to worry about much. The DOJ investigation question came at him early and Mr. Buffett, with graceful aplomb fielded it, gave a satisfactory answer that left his integrity intact, and the crowd satisfied, and then just moved on. Crisis avoided.

For six hours, I sat with my peers taking in the wit and wisdom of one of the icons of industry of our time. Another one of those life experiences that I highly recommend if you ever get the chance.

* * *

"Hey," Wendy interrupted me at the computer. "This is the longest chapter in the book. You already told them about Warren Buffet a couple years ago. This story is getting redundant. Don't you think it is time to move on to something else?"

"Okay," Jon reasonable replied. "Like what?"

"Like anything, but not much of it. Even this book has got to end somewhere. Give them the two best stories from the rest of the year, and let's call it a wrap."

"Are you kidding me? I'm only up to April 30th, 2005."

"Well you just went over seven thousand words for this year's story. You get one more chapter."

"How about one more chapter and an epilogue."

"Okay, but it better be a *DaVinci Code*-sized chapter. Keep it short and on point."

"Only the best stuff. I promise."

Chapter 29

Our One Indulgence

"Hit the deck! Incoming!" I yelled in my sleep as I executed a tuck and roll off my bunk and dug for the dirt.

Boom. Boom. Boom. The string of explosions walked down the river valley towards my location, pinned down in the weeds.

Fissssshhheeuw. The high pitched banshee whine of a rocket launched into the night sky from the bushes 100 meters north of my position. The sound quickly followed by the sharp bang of the warhead detonating.

Proximity fuse set to air burst.

After three days of perpetual bombardment I was getting to be an expert at recognizing the type of weapon by the sound it made. We were deep behind the lines in Indian Country and just trying to keep our heads down and get through the assault unscathed. Coby and I huddled close in our foxhole, waiting for the barrage to stop when our world lit up like a noon-day sun.

"It's July 5th, for Pete's sake," Wendy said as she flipped on the overhead lights in the bedroom of our short-term rental. "When are these idiots going to run out of fireworks? It's midnight already on a work night."

"I didn't even think these things were legal in Maryland," I said, as another stick of cherry bombs exploded two houses over, followed immediately by a fusillade of bottle rockets from the dock on the opposite bank of the creek. A whiff of cordite drifted in our window, kept cracked to keep the room from getting stuffy.

"Where are those stupid earplugs?" Wendy said, closing the window and rooting around in the dresser for some relief.

With ear plugs in, we were finally able to able to get some sleep. With our move less than four weeks away, we needed to conserve our energy, and sleep was already a commodity in short supply in our house.

* * *

When we had first embarked on the adventure of building a new home, in our typical optimistic fashion, we totally underestimated both the time and the expense involved in the project. When our old house in Severna Park sold quickly, we had optimistically rented a house for only nine months. As nine months grew into a year, on it's way to fifteen months, we got an e-mail from the landlord.

"Hope everything is going well with your building project. We had anticipated that you would be out by May, so we've planned to put the house on the market and sell it. Hope you don't mind showing it seven days a week. Also we will be coming through Maryland on our 49-foot trawler and would like to tie up to the dock in the backyard for a month. Hope this doesn't present any problems."

Well, lucky for us all we really liked them, and they liked us. They didn't ask us to leave before we were ready, and we didn't mind having backyard neighbors for the month of May. When one of their waterway acquaintances dropped by for a week in their large cabin cruiser, we had quite a marina going. Including small boats we had almost 200 feet of yacht tied up to our pier complex.

The month flew by and our landlord moved on, and we got down to the final issues with building our house. After meeting with three different low-voltage electrical contractors, I brought the proposals in to the dining area of the rental one evening to lay out the case to my purchasing manager wife.

"I've analyzed the three bids the way you told me. First I graded them on responsiveness to our requests. Then on their responsibility to do the job. Then I evaluated what they were offering for price."

Wendy nodded encouragingly. I was in line with COMAR so far, the Code of Maryland Regulations for procurement.

"The first contractor was a flake. They didn't even know anything about the technology we saw at the National Home Builders Association show in Orlando. I don't have any confidence in their capability to perform and Dave says they only did one small job for them so he doesn't have a good feel for their quality." I paused to throw their proposal away.

"Second contractor was unresponsive to our requests. They only want to sell what they want to sell and that isn't what we want." I shoved their proposal to the side.

"The third contractor seems to know what they are doing and they put a lot of time into their bid."

"What are they going to install for us?" Wendy asked.

"Mainly it's just wire," I replied. "We are trying to keep the price down so I told them not to put in a whole house sound system, so they just pre-wired for it. As far as HDTV, they said the standards haven't been set yet, so they won't give us any TVs or Receivers, but they will run a massive cable from the electrical room to everwhere we might ultimately want TVs. They are going to put three antennas on the roof, plus hook us up to basic cable as well. We won't be able to watch anything, but when the standards for HDTV get set in the next few years, we will be ready whichever way they go. They don't have an alarm system in their bid, but will run some wires for it. Oh, and they have a little panel that will program all the lights in the house to dim with the push of a single button."

"How much?" A skeptical Wendy inquired.

"Only seventy eight thousand dollars."

"No TVs in that price?"

"Correct."

"Speakers? Radios?"

"Nope."

"So, basically, you are telling me that for seventy eight thousand dollars we get some wire in the walls and the lights dim when you push a button."

"Exactly."

"If we don't do this, how do we dim the lights?"

"With the light switches."

"Well, I've got some thoughts but I'm leaving this one to you. I'll handle window treatments. You handle wiring."

I thought about it long and hard. It was a compelling story that with one button I could set the mood for the entire house. Running late for a party? Phone ahead on my cell phone and hit 'Entertainment' and the lights would turn on and dim to the right level, fireplaces would light, music would start playing, and maybe even the oven would warm, although that might have involved a $10,000 up-charge. They were a little vague on that part.

I poured over the plans of the house, computing distances to dim all the lights for a party manually, or turn things off at bedtime. The more I thought about it, the more ludicrous it seemed to run wires for speakers we didn't have and probably wouldn't be getting, and more wires for advanced TVs that might come and go in a generation of technology before we ever actually used the high-tech wiring in the walls. I surfed the internet and put together my alternative plan for Wendy's review.

"I think we should bag the low-voltage stuff entirely," I said, launching into my sales pitch. "I can flip the light switches manually. Instead I have one little indulgence I thing we should get that will fulfill much of what the LutronMan was going to provide at fraction of the cost."

"Oh, this is going to be good," Wendy replied. "One little indulgence?"

"Well, two actually. But it only costs pennies compared to the bid we got for wire. Plus we get immediate satisfaction from it."

"What is it?"

"The first thing is a Baby Grand Player Piano." We'd seen one of these in a small inn in London and had enjoyed listening to Elton John during breakfast. I knew Wendy was predisposed toward the idea and with nine years of piano training in her past, would relish having a nice piano under the roof. With DVD piano rolls available from Mozart to Dueling Banjoes, and everything in between, we should be able to have 'live' music for any occasion.

"Okay," Wendy said cautiously. "What's part two?"

"A levitating plasma TV," I replied. "It sits in a cabinet at the end of the bed in the master bedroom, and with the push of a button it rises up out of the cabinet. When we don't want to watch TV, it drops back down into the cabinet and won't block the view of the water."

"Done."

And with that pronouncement, we wrapped up our 18 month selection process. From door knobs to dining room chandeliers, we had made thousands of decisions. At the end of the day, there is only one thing we would have done differently. In the ten weeks we have lived here we have already build ten years of memories. This house is just a lot of fun and we love sharing it with friends and family. My parents spent two weeks with us in September and had a delightful time entertaining their east coast friends here. We still have a few sticks of furniture on order, and window treatments being manufactured, but if all goes well, we will be all set for the event described in the Epilogue.

If we don't get a chance to say so in person on January 1st, we hope you have a great holiday season, and want to thank you for being part of our life.

Merry Christmas,

Jon & Wendy

Epilogue

Epilogue

The Invitation

We are having a:

Clean Shoes Open House

From

Noon To 6:00 p.m.

On

Sunday, January 1st, 2006

At Our New Home!

We can promise that *Top Gun* will be playing continuously and please bring your swimsuit if you want to try the pool. Oh, yeah: ***Free Elevator Rides!*** But good luck finding the secret passageways. You are on your own there.

Hope to see you on the 1st!

The End

...for now

978-0-595-67576-0
0-595-67576-X

Printed in the United States
40467LVS00004B/133-156